The Seventh Round

A Novel

Alan Wynzel

Kung Fu Treachery Press

Rancho Cucamonga, CA

Copyright © Alan Wynzel, 2020

First Edition 1 3 5 7 9 10 8 6 4 2

ISBN: 978-1-950380-94-7

LCCN: 2020932299

Design, edits and layout: John T. Keehan, Jr.

Cover image: Jon Lee Grafton

Author photo: T. Wynzel

With special thanks to Melvin Litton,
a fellow Warrior of the Word

The Seventh Round

Monday. It's an hour before dawn. The apartment is cold. I haven't turned up the heat yet. I can't afford it. Later on, I will. For now I huddle on the sofa, shivering in an old quilt. The leather sofa is my bed when my kids are here. The leather is hard and cold like the jagged shards of frosted grass outside.

The gun rests in my hands. Also cold and dead. But pregnant with possibilities.

The gun is a .38 caliber revolver with a seven-round cylinder, cast in steel alloy. Rendered in a deep blue unseen in the dark. I feel the heft of it, the solidity of the thing, as I stroke the smooth metal with my fingers and thumbs. I take it in my right hand. A perfect fit, as if custom-made. I finger the trigger and thumb the hammer. I never gave much thought to guns before, but now I understand. The shape, the weight, the easy fit in the hand. The power inherent. The potential. The gun forge may follow the blueprint, but the design was cast from the base yearnings of the soul.

I open and spin the empty cylinder. The action is even, fluid. It shuts with a soft click. I haven't loaded it yet. It isn't time.

I have to get up now. I wrap the gun in a hand towel and, feeling my way in the darkness, slide it with a tinkling of glass behind the bottles of vodka, gin, and tequila in the liquor cabinet. I set it beside the box of shells. Withdrawing my hand, I tip the gin bottle, and catch it just by instinct. I'm well accustomed with handling those bottles in the dark.

Now into the kitchen, where I shut the louvered door behind me, turn on the light, and put water on for coffee. In silence, I will have breakfast then tiptoe to the toilet for an hour-long struggle to clear my bleeding bowels, a task never completed, and finished with the painstaking easing of my screaming hemorrhoids back inside myself. Holding my breath and praying that they don't rupture completely. When that is all done, I will turn on the heat, awaken my kids and take them to school. Then I will go to work.

I will leave the gun here, for now.

*   *   *

My kids are quiet. They usually aren't. Maybe they are because I was different this weekend. I kept my distance. That's not the way I am. We're very close. My son is thirteen and my daughter eleven. They tried to engage me, to play, to joke, but I would only go so far. I always try to do things with them. But not this time. So they found things to do on their own. They gave up on me.

It's better that they do.

They eat their breakfast in front of the television. I don't usually let them, it slows them down. Today is different. Like me. I am different. And they know it.

I embrace and kiss them in the frozen parking lot, atop the blackened ice. I do it at home because it would embarrass them at school. Tonight they go back to their mother and I'm not due to have them until next week.

I tell them that I love them. That hasn't changed. And it never will.

The car is cold and the highway is black and the sky is gray. Eight quick miles to school, in silence. Questioning looks. Concern. Dad is different now. Yes I am, because I have a gun and a box of shells hidden in the liquor cabinet.

And a plan.

But Dad still loves you.

I come more alive when they leave. I smile broadly and wish them a good day and a good week and I'll miss you. I don't want to leave them disconcerted. They seem reassured. Then they're gone, into their own world, the world of school, where they will rehearse for Life.

It will be a poor preparation.

I skid onto the highway, cut across four lanes, and in another mile, make my exit. Gray flurries drift across the road. I pull off into the office park, formerly a swamp, now drained and filled with a base of stone, paved and capped with turf and steel, brick and asphalt. A reeking bog transformed into a center of human enterprise. But a new stench lingers here.

Dust and flurries swirl in the parking lot. I park, and the wind rocks my car. I grab my case and hurriedly make for the ground level parking deck, open to the lot. The icy wind infiltrates my cuffs and collar and runs along my trembling skin like cold water. The deck is reserved for the executives of the various companies occupying the building. I can't park there, but I can find some shelter from the wind, and I can smoke there.

I avoid the three strangers from another company huddled over the ash can, shivering as they smoke and watch the flurries blow past. I crouch behind a pillar but it still takes 3 matches to light up. The damn wind. But I'm in no hurry. I have time.

I take slow drags and watch as more cars arrive, park, and the people dash inside. I work with a few of them.

This is my second time working here. I'm a database programmer, and have been, for fifteen years. I worked four years in my first stint in the company, and they laid me off, along with nearly half of the technology group. The company had been bought a few years prior by venture capitalists, who, having milked it dry in a few short years, had no use for it anymore. So they cut staff to show a profit in order to sell it. They used the Great Recession as an excuse, but we all knew better. I was out of work for a year and a half. I could barely get an interview. I'm obsolete, now. I don't know the new technologies, and I couldn't find anything I was qualified for.

A few months ago, my boss called me back to work. The best people remaining in our group had found jobs elsewhere. The few remaining were not enough to keep things going. My boss was desperate. And so was I. But they took advantage of me. They made me a Temp. No more salary; instead, I get paid by the hour. If I take time off, I don't get paid. Not even for holidays. And no benefits. I haven't had health insurance in a long time.

But I had no choice. I had to take what they gave me.

I don't like to be without choices.

Len comes sprinting into the deck. We work together. We smoke together. His red hands shake as he struggles to light up.

"Fucking weather!" he says.

"Yup."

He coughs and spits onto the deck. It splatters in a red and yellow Rorschach pattern.

Cancer? TB? What do you think, doctor?

"I hear they're gonna make the announcement today," Len says.

He means our layoff notice. The final notice. The company was finally acquired by a competitor two months ago. I've been transferring data files to the buyer every day since. There isn't much left to send.

"Oh yeah?"

Len's face is red and creased with worry. His eyes tremble with fear. He didn't get laid off with me, but he couldn't find anything else in the meantime. He too, is obsolete.

I'm not worried anymore.

"Yeah. There'll be a meeting called. You'll see."

I believe him. Len has a connection upstairs who makes predictions. They all come true.

"This is it," he groans. "This is finally it."

"Don't worry about it."

His eyes seem to dislocate from their sockets. "What the fuck do you mean, don't worry about it? We're gonna lose our fucking jobs! And there's nothing out there for us! We're almost fifty years old!"

"How do you get your eyes to do that?"

"What? What the fuck are you talking about? How are we gonna live on Unemployment? You went broke and bankrupt on it. And what are we gonna do when it runs out, deliver newspapers? Pump gas? Manage the hardware department at Wal-Mart?"

Len is a bit high-strung. But he's a good guy.

"It'll be okay, Len. You have nothing to worry about."

Len eyes me with care.

"That can't be a cigarette you're smoking, man. It must be something from the Sixties."

I chuckle.

"Let's get inside, I'm fucking freezing and I need some fucking coffee."

"Yeah, me too."

We drop our coats and bags in our cubes. Our colleagues are coming in, milling about without aim. It's not the typical Monday morning reluctance and confusion. They are scared. Len doesn't have a monopoly on inside information, apparently.

We pour coffees and sip them in his cube. We are not working. We don't speak. Then I excuse myself. Coffee makes me shit. It takes a half an hour. Blood and piles again. I wait until the men's room is empty before I emerge from the stall to wash. I want no witness to my bloodstained hands. I've struggled with this for ten years now; strained to stop the bleeding and to find some meaning in the metaphor. No crime or guilt to which it should apply. I stare at my hands. The stains will not quit the cuticles of my fingers. I scrub them clean with the frenzy of Macbeth.

This is my oracle.

*   *   *

Ted sits across from me.

"Where the fuck you been?"

Ted's nearly retired. He was laid off with me the first time. They brought him back, too.

"Whaddaya mean?" I smile.

"You dropped off your shit and disappeared for an hour. I'm bored."

He fires a rubber band at me. It hits me on the chin. I shoot one back. I miss. We do this all the time.

Ted is also a good guy.

"If this were a real job, you'd be fired for all your disappearances."

"But it isn't, so who gives a fuck."

"That's right. Besides, we're temps."

They're taking advantage of Ted, too. But he has a wife with a good job and money in the bank so it doesn't matter much. He's just here for fun.

"So I hear there may be some shit going down today," he says.

"So I heard."

"So what are you gonna do?"

He cares. He worries about me.

"I'm gonna do what I have to do."

"What, size up refrigerator boxes to use as your next apartment?"

"I was thinking I'd pimp you out for back alley blowjobs. But it has to be a dark alley so they can't see your ugly mug."

"Prick!" He lets fly with another rubber band. It strikes right between my eyes. We laugh like hell.

I will miss Ted.

*   *   *

I transfer some data files to the buyer. At this rate of transmission, I'll be done in two weeks. There won't be anything left to do after that. Most people in the group have already stopped working. There is nothing for them to do anymore.

Ted fires off a few more volleys of rubber while I'm working, but I don't respond. I could, but I want to finish. I don't like leaving things undone. He gives up after a while and takes an early lunch.

Then I'm done, and can't do anything until I receive further instruction on the details of the next batch. I throw on my coat, take my lunch bag and head outside. The wind has passed. But the gray lid of cloud remains, pressing down on the scene. I get in my car and take the drive to another office building, and park in its lot. I want to get away, and this is as far as I can go, in the time that I have.

My lunch is a can of vegetable soup and a bologna sandwich. I yank the lid from the can and soup splatters on my leather coat. I sop up the red beads of broth with my fingers and lick them clean. I eat the soup cold with a plastic spoon. I sip the dregs of broth from the can, careful of the sharp rim pressing on my lips. I eat the sandwich, chewing slowly, while I watch a heron, perched gracefully on a broken limb overhanging a nearby man-made pond. The bird looks confused. It suddenly flies off. I shut my eyes and try to sleep. I think of my kids. Soon it's time to go back.

There's an email waiting for me. The same email waiting for all of us. We must report to the boardroom at three-thirty.

I can hear anguished whisperings all around me.

Len appears, wild-eyed and trembling.

"This is it. This is fucking it!"

He's in his coat, and reeks of smoke, but I suggest another cigarette.

"Sure," he says.

We go down to the deck. Most of the smokers in what remains of our company are clustered behind a pylon, puffing, wringing their hands, and shaking their heads. Because most of them are obsolete, too. And if they're not, the Great Recession still holds sway, with no end in sight.

"This is it!" Len shouts. There is some laughter. Len likes to perform, and everyone knows it.

I stand on the edge of the group, in silence, content to savor the taste of my cigarette. Len goes on, and the others join in, and soon, the deck rings with an agitated, incomprehensible babble.

Nanette, an older woman in Technology, turns to me.

"You're pretty quiet about all this. What do you think? This is the second time around for you."

"What?"

"I said this is the second time for you. You paying attention to any of this?"

"No, sorry. I was thinking about cigarettes."

"Cigarettes?"

"Yes. I read that some cultures consider cigarettes the food of the soul. I just can't remember what culture."

"You're weirder than normal today."

She turns back to the others.

At three-thirty we file slowly upstairs and settle anxiously in the boardroom, where extra seats have thoughtfully been brought in. The seats are soon filled, but not the room—not many people left in the company. The president takes the podium and with sincere regrets tells us what we already knew: In thirty days we're closing down. Your managers will meet with you regarding your severance very soon (does not apply to Temps). You've done a great job. I am proud to have worked with you. Good luck to you all.

Of course the president has a new job with the company that bought us, along with a large bonus for managing the transition.

No one says anything about it.

Wasn't it our fathers and grandfathers who plunged ashore on Pacific islands, through cyclones of flying steel, to storm Jap bunkers, to scale Suribachi and plant our flag? Wasn't it they who rose from the bloody tideline of Omaha Beach to breach Hitler's Atlantic Wall and liberate Europe? Didn't our mothers and grandmothers labor overtime to forge our arsenal of Democracy, and stood firm despite their grief when the dreaded cables came, bearing regrets and gratitude for their loss?

Their generation did these things, but we are not of their lineage. We are their foster children of some mongrel breed of cowards. Their lineage is as lost as that heron at the pond, drawn here by memory and the lingering scent of this plowed-over swamp over which we play out this drama. Because men came and seized our livelihood and bled it dry to fill their pockets and then cast the empty vessel, and us, aside; and the sonofabitch who turned on us and helped them is rewarded with a fat bonus for tossing us out on the street.

And nobody calls him out on it.

There is some chatter and hand-shaking and ass-kissing, but most of us file quickly from the boardroom and head back downstairs. Len and I go down to the parking garage for a smoke. His eyes are watered; he pretends it's from the smoke and the harsh wind. Other smokers from the company join us. There isn't much talking. I'm asked a few questions about filing for Unemployment, since I've done it already and know the ropes. I'm a veteran. Pin a campaign medal on my chest. Maybe I can pawn it for a week of groceries.

The elevator opens and the president appears. He makes for his company car, a sparkling black Cadillac. When the venture capital firm took over the company, all the executives were directed to purchase a car for their use. But it had to be an American car, because the firm was patriotic, and supported American business and the American Way. So read the memo distributed to the rank-and-file at the time. I wasn't here then, but I found a yellowed copy tacked to a bulletin board in a long-abandoned conference room. The room was being used to store old fixtures and furniture. I was there looking for a replacement for my broken chair.

The president glances our way and nods, barely. He gets in his Caddy and starts it with a roar and I wonder if he's thinking, "Whew, dodged two bullets today—the meeting and running the smoker's gauntlet afterwards."

But I don't think so. He knows us. He's not worried. I believe he really does feel bad for us. And he probably will feel bad a few minutes longer until his cell phone rings or someone cuts him off in traffic on the way home.

Now he's gone and that's the signal. We're done. The cigarettes are twisted into the ashtrays or ground hissing beneath our heels. All but Len's. He flicks his violently at the drifting wake of mist left behind by the Caddy.

"Bastard," he mutters.

We all go home.

*　　*　　*

At home I'm tired but I plunge into my neglected workout routine. Pushups, dumbbell presses, crunches, curls, and bicycles for the abs. I need to be in shape.

When I'm done I drop two cans of beans, some tomato puree and hot sauce in a pot and set it to simmer. Then I throw on torn jeans and a sweater and my old leather coat and head outside for a cigarette. I go through the parking lot and on to the cul-de-sac. I peer into the trees ringing the paved semi-circle. An assortment of homeless men have lived in these woods. They creep in late at night and scurry uptown at dawn. I've seen some of them while I've been out on the front stoop of my apartment drinking. They look down at the ground and try to be invisible as they pass. They step lightly in the trees, silently, so as not to disturb. They feign nonexistence.

I imagine the tall lean one was once an executive. But his company was top-heavy, so he had to go. His house was foreclosed on so he took to drinking and his wife and kids left him. When the house was gone he wound up on the street. The stocky dark one was a fry cook, always just getting by, and when the restaurant shut down it was a quick fall for him. And the one with the wild mane of hair and shaggy beard who mutters to himself, he's just a madman. But what was he before he was a madman?

But there is no sign of them now. The black trees are still and the light crust of snow is only broken by deer tracks. Where are they?

They all came to this street for a while. And now I'm on this street for a while. But I won't take to the woods.

Never.

My fingers are burning with cold when I step back inside. The rich smell that fills the apartment tells me the beans are done. I'm starving. I toss a salad while the beans cool and then ladle some into a pair of soft tortilla wraps. I eat. But I can barely taste it. I've had it a hundred times before. After dinner, I have instant coffee and another cigarette. It's dark by then.

                    *   *   *

It's much later. I'm in the easy chair. It's dark. I've gone through two gin and tonics and one CD. Now the player is silent. I sip my drink and the ice rattles in the glass.

The gun is in my hand. The box of shells sits on the coffee table before me. I pry it open and take one round from the box. It's cold and hard. I feel my way along the smooth jacket, working my fingers up to the hard, pointed nose. I consider the things this small piece of metal can do. How it penetrates to the heart of things. How it reduces, resolves, finalizes. Vengeance, faithlessness, honor. All can be redressed, or achieved, with this little bit of steel.

I break open the cylinder and work the round into the chamber. I spin it once and snap it back into place. It makes a clack that rings in the silence like one short step toward resolution.

There is only one shell in the gun but it feels heavier. That much more weight to add to my momentum.

Not too fast, now. I put the gun and the shells carefully away. It's loaded, now. Anything could happen.

I put the gin away, too. Gin is aromatic, savory. It's mellow and reflective. But now I want to party. I take out the vodka and fill half a glass. I top it off with tonic. Just a little taste, I say. I say it out loud to myself, "Just a little taste". And then I say, "It's too fucking quiet in here". I rummage through my CDs for something raucous. I pick a Stooges album and put it on the tinny player. Soon it's playing, and I sit in my chair and listen, sucking at my vodka, and I have my party for a while.

When the Stooges are done I shut off the player. I am not drunk. That was not my intent, and I have remained true to it. Tomorrow I will go back to work and when it is done it will be one day closer to the end of my tenure there. I'm very tired just thinking about it. I will be glad when it's done, I think. I just want to get it over with.

I've done all I can tonight. I go to bed.

*   *   *

I don't sleep well in my bed. It makes me see things in dreams that I don't want to see anymore.

I took the bed from my house when I got divorced. My wife and I slept in it in the last few years of our marriage. I took it to my first bachelor apartment, and I had no problem sleeping on it. No sorrows, no sentiments, no associations. I took a few other women to bed in it. Pull back the sheet and you can read in the brown and oval stains the story of the denouement of my marriage and the sex and brief infatuations that followed.

The bed was fine for a few years like this.

Then I met Johanna and fell in love again. We wrote a new story in the bed to overlay the old, in human ink and in whispers: "I never loved anyone as much as you." We took the bed as ours when we shared a home, along with her two kids and mine. But it fell apart before it even started. We were great lovers, but we could not live together. We could find joy only in the bed, and out of it, not much more than sorrow. She didn't want me there, and soon, I didn't want to be there. In the midst of this, I lost my job. Money soon became a problem. I went bankrupt. Break up, reconciliation, infidelity and reconciliation again; finally, she told me to go. That was a year ago. I came here and brought the bed with me. I was glad to go and it was fine for a while. A brief vignette with another woman, done before the ink dried, was written not long after. And then I settled into the bed, alone.

And then the dreams began. Johanna came to me.

I thought I hated her. And I suppose I do. But I can't stop loving her, either. She comes to me, or I bring her, and does it matter? She is here, and I make love to her in my dreams. But there is no joy in it. There is me, and Johanna, and an awful space between.

I can't sleep well anymore unless I'm dead drunk. And tonight I am not. I'm awake in the frozen dark, panting and sweating from an unbearable flush of heat. I toss the quilt aside for relief.

Later, when I calm down, I know that I have to get her back. And if I can't, I have to settle this once and for all.

II.

Now it's Tuesday morning. I'm slow and fuzzy from the drinking and the lost sleep. But it's no hangover.

I take my time getting ready. I read a book while I sit on the toilet oozing blood. But I don't think about it. I enjoy the book. Then I shower, dress, and pass outside into the bright, frosty air. There are only two other cars in the lot besides mine. Eight apartments: one resident leaving, two staying in today. One car belongs to the old retired guy who is drinks too much to drive anymore. He takes cabs uptown every day at midmorning to make the bars when they open. The other belongs to one of the young, pretty girls next door to mine. Just the thought of them arouses me. I laugh to myself, amused at the stirring in my pants. I'm nearly twenty years older than them.

I'm not going straight to work. I'm not worried, they won't fire me. They still need a little more work from me, and no one else can do it.

Instead I go to the Unemployment office uptown. I have to ask a question, although I'm sure I know the answer.

The woman at the desk there has always been helpful, and knowledgeable. Today is no different. She gives me my answer. I smile and thank her, and there is pity in her eyes. I wouldn't want her job.

I show up at work an hour late. But is there such a thing as being late, when it's all over anyway? My boss sees me coming in and doesn't say anything. People are drinking coffee and talking quietly in small groups, and some are even working. Ted is playing solitaire on his computer.

"Where ya been?"

"Fucking your mom."

He laughs.

"No you haven't. She may be senile, but she's not blind."

Now I laugh.

"So that's it," he says. "In a month we'll be free."

"Yes, we will."

"So what are you gonna do?"

I shrug. "You?"

"Well, get my boat ready for Spring. Work on the house. Try to ride the Unemployment until sixty-two, and then take Social Security."

"You take it so early you won't get much."

"True, and that sucks, but it's better than getting nothing. What am I going to do, wait three more years, with no income at all? I'm not going to find a job at my age. I'll take it early and the wife will retire soon, she's got thirty years in, and we'll sell the house, if we can. Hopefully the market picks up so we can at least break even. Head South, find a place on the water. "

"It'll work out for you."

"I hope. Looking for a job?"

"Of course."

"Anything?"

"Same like every day."

The phone rings. It's Len.

"Smoke?"

"Sure. Be down in a minute."

"Your boyfriend?" says Ted.

"Yup. Wanna come to our circle-jerk? You can have the middle. I promise not to miss."

"I promise not to miss," he says, and hits me with a rubber band in the chest.

Len is already downstairs in the parking garage. I try to convince him to go outside, in the sun.

"But it's fucking cold out there."

"Well, it's cold here too. It's open to the air. Probably colder, it never gets the sun."

I can't convince him. So we shiver in the gloom.

"What the fuck am I going to do," he says. "I'm in the same boat as you. I'm not gonna find a job. My mortgage is more than Unemployment pays. My wife works but that barely covers the bills. Shit."

He takes a long drag on his cigarette and then begins to chew on his fingers, spitting bits of skin on the deck.

"I just look at how long you were out of work last time and I think, I can't do that, I won't be able to make it."

"I didn't make it either," I say.

"Maybe I can go to school and drive a truck or something. Or paint houses. Fuck. Twenty years in a fucking career and it doesn't count for anything. I'm back to square one."

"You'll have some time. You're getting a severance. That will tide you over for a while."

"I suppose. You getting anything?"

"No, I got mine last time. It wasn't much, I wasn't here long enough."

"Shit. What are you going to do?"

"What I gotta do. My old man used to say, 'A man's gotta do what a man's gotta do.' And then my mother would belt him one."

"That's nice. Seriously, you have any ideas? I need some ideas."

"I have an idea."

"What?"

"It's a secret."

"Yeah, sure. You don't have a clue, either."

We grind out our cigarettes and light another. We smoke this one in silence. Ron from our group joins us. He never says much. He merely nods and lights up.

It's a brief, comfortable silence. But I'd rather be outside in the sun.

Back at my desk, there is work to do. I have to transfer

an enormous amount of files in a single batch. But first I have to make a complicated change to the record layout. I work on that for a few hours. In between, I pause to look at the job boards on the Internet. And I think about Johanna. Ted tries to play around, he shoots more rubber bands, but I ignore him.

I break for lunch. I'm hungry, but I force myself to walk in the sunshine first. I want to catch it while it lasts. It warms my face. I find myself smiling, if just for a moment.

Back at the building, I pause for a cigarette. No one I know is around. It's just as well. I don't want to talk to anyone.

I eat at my desk. The place is empty. The day after the notice, and everyone is out for a long lunch. Some will be having drinks.

I would like a drink.

Soup again, today, cold from the can. And a pair of cold hot dogs. I could microwave it all, but I don't feel like walking down the hall to the break room. I eat it slowly while working on the program to create the files.

It takes another hour to finish the coding. Then I create a few files to test it. They look good. At this point I pour a coffee so I can crap soon. While the coffee cools, I prepare a document to submit my changes and create the real files. I email it to the Quality group—they must review my work and approve the changes. When I'm done, I drink my coffee. Len and five of the others return from their long lunch. I should have gone, they say. Yes, I should have, I think, because they all smell like liquor. Except for Len, who had pancreatitis and can't drink anymore. Although I think he should. It might make him happy again.

He wants to go smoke, but I decline. I tell him I'm too busy for a break. The truth is, it's time to crap. I sneak away when he's gone.

When I'm back, angrily picking at the crimson stains on my cuticles, there is an email waiting for me. It's from Nanette, the head of the Quality group. She wants to see me about my changes and the files.

And then Ted says, "Nanette was looking for you."

"Fuck," I say.

"What did you do wrong this time?"

"I was born."

Ted cackles. But it's not funny.

Nanette is very particular about details. From the perspective of programmers, like myself, the Quality group exists merely to test our work and ensure we didn't make any programming mistakes. We just want to get our code pushed through and get the job done. But, for Quality, it's much more than that. Politics play into it. Quality sees their job as much more than testing and fixing mistakes. They see themselves as upholders of company policy. They look to see if we've done our work according to the rules. They also constantly look to see how we can enhance our work, with long term improvements and efficiencies in mind. None of this is wrong or bad—except that when they get their way, we wind up doing our work twice. They will answer that we should have done it right the first time. Unfortunately, when the customer, or the management, is screaming for their files or for something to be fixed in a hurry, that is impossible.

Nanette is notorious for doing it Quality's way. She's fought it out with all of us, and me, in particular.

I dread going to see her, but I have to get those files out, so I hurry to her office to get it over with.

"About these changes," she begins, without a greeting. That and her tone tell me we're in for a fight.

I sit down. "What is it?" I grunt.

She looks at me, surprised. I am usually friendly and agreeable. I always have been with her, in the hopes of charming her into not breaking my balls.

The questions begin. Why did I do it this way—was I thinking about X, Y, and Z? Do we know what the consequences could be? Why do they want the file this way? Does Carl (my manager) know you're doing it this way?

She goes on. I'm very angry. Why does it always have to be this way with her? Why does she have to use this power to obstruct me? Just because she can?

"Look," I say, and wave my arm across her desk. "Enough already. I have one answer for all your questions. These files are for the buyer. They bought us, we work for them, and this is what they want. Case closed."

Her back stiffens and her eyes narrow. My ex-wife used to do that.

"I understand that. But I don't want to set a precedent for allowing sloppy, ill-considered procedures. I have to consider the consequences in the future."

"Nanette," I whisper, "what future?"

She looks down and toys with the printout of my request. Then she looks up at me and very calmly, says, "That doesn't matter. I'm going to do my job the right way, whether we're here another week or ten more years."

Of course, I think. This is all she has. She's almost sixty and there is an Internet job board on her computer displaying an empty search return.

I reach out and take the printout.

"I'll go back and fix it," I say.

Back at my cube, Ted looks up from his game of solitaire.

"So? Back to the drawing board, I presume?"

"Yeah."

"You should have offered your firstborn."

"Never mind."

I sit down and consider how I can fix the code to satisfy Nanette. A few minutes later, she appears, with my request in her hand.

"Are you making the changes I asked for?"

"Yes," I say.

"Don't. Just have Carl sign off that it's OK the way you did it. If he does, I'll push it through this afternoon."

"OK. Thanks."

Ted is watching. When Nanette is gone, he shakes his head.

"I wouldn't have believed it if I hadn't seen it myself," he says.

"First time for everything."

"Yeah. Except the first time you get laid. When's that gonna happen?"

"Shut up, old man."

Carl signs off on it, of course. And then curses out Nanette, like he always does when we have problems with her, and only half in jest. But I don't join in, this time.

The job to create the files kicks off before the end of the day. It will take a few days to run, but the buyer will get their files by the end of the week.

I came in at ten, and I should stay until six. But I leave at four.

I don't have any more work.

*   *   *

I eat the leftover beans for dinner. A flavored bulk to fill my empty stomach with protein, fiber, and carbohydrates. A green salad for vitamins. A fill up for the organic machine. A brief chore, like gassing up my car. A reduction to the essentials. Then coffee and a cigarette, to help evacuate the waste from last night's meal. Input and output, and to what end?

It's bitter cold outside. Today's bright sun heralded an Arctic front, clear and frozen hard. I clutch the hot mug of coffee in my bare hand, my cigarette in the other, and switch them back and forth, trying to keep my fingers warm. I check the trees for human tracks, but there are none. A man would freeze to death in the woods at night without a fire. And maybe even with one.

Later, I am restless. There are things in my mind that want my attention, and I don't want to give it to them. I can hear their murmuring demands in my head. I'm sick of thinking of things. When I think about them, I have to confront them. I pace back and forth through the apartment, trying to shake them.

"I just don't want to deal with it," I say aloud. "I'm sick of all these problems, and I'm sick of feeling like shit all the time."

I have to get away. And I do know how. But I'm reluctant, because it's such an awful waste.

But I give in. I gather the lotion, a towel, and my glasses. I shut off the lights and turn up the heat a fraction. It's a routine, like cooking beans. I've done it a thousand times before.

I will surf porn and masturbate tonight. I will sit before the laptop, pants curled around my ankles, and stroke myself for hours, working it time and again to the brink of climax until I can't take it anymore. Then, in an ecstasy of fantasy and lust, I'll stare down the slutty bitch filling the screen with her provocative flesh and cum in my hand and all over myself until there's no cum left. And in the spent aftermath of shame I'll drag myself up on stiff, cold legs, wash myself, piss painfully, and put my pants back on.

I can't help myself, and I can't stop myself. So I do it.

Four hours later, I'm done. It's nearly midnight. My cock is raw, my palm aches and my legs are shaking. My ass aches from the hard kitchen chair. And the fan in my laptop is whirring loudly as it frantically tries to cool down the hard drive. I shut the machine off. Let the damn thing rest.

And now I feel the shame that I always do. Not over the porn and the sex. Shame and regret for all the lost time. And maybe, I think, shame at taking pleasure for myself, when there's so much that needs to be done. I laugh to myself—this isn't a Catholic guilt, it's more a Protestant Work Ethic guilt. This is all the more amusing, as I'm a Jew.

At least I didn't have to think for four hours. I shut down all the thoughts in my head for a while.

But that's done and now I have to consider what I found out in the Unemployment office this morning: when the layoff comes, I'll still be considered to be on my previous Unemployment claim. I haven't been back on my job long enough to qualify for filing a new claim. And my old claim has just sixty days of benefits remaining.

Sixty days after the layoff, I won't have an income.

My bank account is empty.

My skills are obsolete.

I'm forty-seven.

What will I be eating then? I'm already down to beans, sardines, and cheap hot dogs. And my voicemail is already filling up with messages looking for credit card and car payments.

They are still saying "please". What will they be saying then?

I get the .38 and the shells, jam a second round in the cylinder and slap it shut. I don't pause this time to relish the feeling or the weight or the inherent potential. I know what it can do.

III.

Wednesday is different. I bring the gun to work in my coat pocket.

I want to get used to carrying it, but this is harder than I think. First I put it in the right pocket with my keys. That makes sense because I'm right-handed. But then my right side is too heavy, and the keys clatter against the gun. So I try my left pocket, but that doesn't work either as it bangs against my cell phone. I'm afraid the hard steel of the gun will crack the phone. I don't want to change the coat pocket system I've used for years, but in the end I reason it's justified. I put the gun in my right-hand pocket, the keys in my left-hand pocket (which is awkward when starting my car since the ignition switch is on the right side of the steering column) and the cell phone in my left pants pocket. To do that I have to move the hemorrhoid ointment I carry hidden to work from my left to my right pants pocket. Moving the ointment doesn't bother me, but I really want to keep the phone on my left. I don't want to completely fuck up my set ways.

Not that it matters anymore. And it's good to step out of my comfort zone, I think.

And so I arrive at work with two secrets in my pockets: a gun and a tube of hemorrhoid ointment.

I wish I could tell someone.

"Hey, Ted," I say when I reach my cube.

"What?"

I shove my hands in my coat pockets and pitch a tent over my crotch with my fists.

"Do Mae West for me," I say.

"Huh?"

"Mae West! Christ, you're a fucking idiot. Is that a gun in your pocket, or are you just glad to see me?"

"Huh! Well I know that sure as hell isn't your little dick."

"You're right!" I say, and then I hang up my coat. That's as far as I dare go.

Ted shakes his head. "Drinking last night?"

"No, I was beating off for four hours."

"Right. You couldn't keep that thing of yours up for four minutes."

"Your wife would tell you different."

"If you have to settle for fucking my wife, you're a complete loser."

He won that one. That's fine.

I log on to my computer and check the file job. It's moving along. The buyer has received some of the files, and the rest are in progress. There's nothing for me to do except monitor the job until it's done.

I go for a smoke with Len. We join a few others on the deck. I bury my free hand in my pocket and secretly fondle the gun. I feel like I'm getting away with something. I feel like I'm better than the others. It makes me feel good.

Len has nothing to say today. That isn't like him. I wonder if he has anything in his coat pocket.

When I return I check my personal email, my bank statement, and the job boards. I've been looking for a job for so long I recognize all the catch phrases for the technical requirements and experience. I can easily see what jobs I'm not qualified for—with some, it's as simple as the title of the position. With most, I have to look with a bit more care, although usually not much beyond the first sentence.

I'm almost done with the current daily listings when I stop. I feel like I ran over something in the road that wasn't a bump. Do I keep going, or back up and look?

I scroll back to one item and read it slowly this time. It's for a long-term contract at an unnamed pharmaceutical company, located nearby. The technical requirements are, surprisingly, exactly what I know and nothing more. An hourly rate is listed, fairly low, but that could work in my favor—I'm desperate enough to take something others might not settle for. The job is listed by a recruiting agency and the contact recruiter is "Bob Smith".

I know it's not "Bob Smith". It's an Indian using an American name to build his business.

But I email my resume anyway. "Bob Smith" calls me twenty minutes later. He is an Indian, and I can barely understand him. I'm tempted to hang up, because I've been down this road before—there is no way this incomprehensible poseur has a preferred vendor status to find job candidates for a major pharmaceutical company. But I go through the motions because I have nothing else to do and no other prospects. I confirm the rate as acceptable. I confirm my availability and my experience. He, in turn, tells me nothing about the company or the project.

"We see first if they want interview."

"Okay, Bob, call me if they do." I hang up.

"Got a job lined up?" Ted says.

"Yeah, a blowjob, like all the others."

"Where?"

"Pharma. Close by."

"He Indian?"

"Yup."

I tell Len about it.

"They're wasting your fucking time," he says.

"I know. But I have time to waste."

I'm surprised when Bob Smith calls me back after lunch.

"You have technical interview tomorrow at two. Can you be available?"

For most technology positions, candidates must first undergo a technical screening in order to assess their knowledge level. They are usually done over the phone. He gives me the name of the technical lead who will conduct the interview—another Indian, but this one, at least, uses his real name. He gives me the name of the company—a big one, the one that everyone wants to get into, but no one can.

I ask him for more specifics on what they need, technically, but he doesn't know. He reads aloud the requirement from the online posting, which doesn't help at all.

I go out for a smoke with Len.

"That guy got me a tech screening for tomorrow. I have to study tonight."

"Study what?"

"Everything. He doesn't know what they want."

"Jesus Christ. That's like being told to prepare for an exam on World History--all of it. How do they expect you to pass like that?"

"I don't know."

"Fuck these Indians. First they come over by the thousands and take over the technology jobs. They get themselves into positions where they can do the tech interviews, and shut out all the Americans. Now they're taking over the goddamn recruiting, too. What kind of country allows this to happen to its workers?"

Len chews on his fingers, spits, and takes a long drag on his cigarette.

What he says is essentially true. It began with the Y2K scare—which was a scam, mostly, an hysteria whipped up by American consulting companies to make a killing charging outrageous rates to place consultants in all the companies desperate to fix their Y2K bugs. I know, because I had a few of those consulting gigs. The consulting companies got rich at the expense of a lot of companies who realized they could no longer afford, or didn't want to spend, the money it took to maintain their software. So they went crying to the government for cheap labor. The lobbyists and campaign contributions did their work and the government took the lid off the restriction on foreign technical workers. American companies were soon flooded with Indians and other foreigners with Bachelor's and Master's in Computer Science or Engineering, who couldn't find jobs at home and were willing to work in America, cheap.

Corporate America got their technology costs under control. The Indians were smart and hard-working. And yes, they do help one another. The companies were happy with them and the low-cost quality they brought to their organizations. And soon the companies realized something else: they could cut their training budgets, too. Before Y2K most companies would train their own staff when they updated their technologies. But with the flood of Indians trained in cutting-edge software, that wasn't necessary anymore. People like me, who learned the rudiments of programming at a six-month program at a technical school (after I couldn't get anywhere in life with my B.A. in Economics) can't compete at all with their education. And without the corporate training, we've become obsolete.

A few others from the group have joined us. But no Indians; none of them smoke. They're too busy working. Len tells them about my impending interview and is soon railing on and on about the injustice of the Indian Takeover. When he pauses for breath, the others hold forth, briefly, until Len picks up again where he left off.

"And of course," he says, "when we had the layoff last time, none of the Indians got laid off. Not one! Management loves them. And who were the only ones who managed to find jobs afterwards? Indians!"

Yes, it's all true. But not as one-sided as it sounds.

"You know what?" I say. "Good for them."

Everyone thinks I'm being sarcastic, but I'm not.

"Listen to me. Sure, the Indians came over and stole our jobs. But we didn't say a word when the government let them into the country to compete with us. And, guess what? While we were busy drinking coffee, going out to smoke, and taking long lunches, they were working hard and they kicked our asses and took over. And we let them."

Nobody likes that. But I don't care. We are not the Omaha Beach generation, and we're paying for it, and somebody should say so.

The conversation drifts onto other topics, revolving around the layoff. What kind of severance are we getting? How do you file for Unemployment? Do you have to prove you're looking for a job? And so on.

I don't pay much attention. I have most of the Unemployment answers, but I don't feel like answering. I'm trying to figure out what I should study for tomorrow. I put out my cigarette and step quietly away.

There are online study guides for interviews, and I find a few that I've used before. I spend the rest of the afternoon alternating between reviewing code, and checking on the file job. The job is fine, but studying is difficult. There is so much to cover, and so many things I could be asked. And a lot that I don't know. This is nothing new to me. I've been embarrassed on plenty of interviews for my lack of knowledge. I don't think this time will be any different. I'm filled with a sense of hopelessness, a hollow, lonely pain, one that I've felt for a long time. I debate cancelling the interview and saving myself all this grief. Why should I keep tilting at windmills? I have other plans, and they don't include a new job.

But I keep at it. I suppose it's pride. I have to feel like I tried, all the way until the end.

Soon it's time to go home. I print out a few sample exams to take with me

*   *   *

When I get home, I'm in a panic. I'm shaking and my heart is pounding. I don't know why. I've had this happen before, and then, too, without any clear reason. I sit down, then I get up, then sit down again. I go outside for a cigarette but have no taste for one, so instead I take slow, long breaths of the cold air and look at the darkening sky and the trees. I grip the gun tight in my pocket. After a while I calm down somewhat, but I don't feel complete. I feel tilted off to one side. Not to the right and not to the left, but over something. A deep pit.

I suddenly have to call my kids. I want to hear their voices. I hurry to the phone and feel the panic rising again. I dial and when my ex-wife picks up I fight to sound calm.

"Hey, I just wanted to say hi to the kids."

"Sure," she says. "But we're about to eat dinner."

Fuck your slop, bitch, this is more important!

"It'll just take a minute."

"Guys! Your Dad's on the phone!"

They pick up on the two extensions simultaneously. My chest is pounding and I feel like I'm about to pitch forward into a hole. I grip the arm of the easy chair for balance.

"Hi, Dad."

"Hi Daddy."

"Hey guys. Just wanted to say hello. How was school?"

"Good."

"OK."

"Have a lot of homework this week?"

"Some."

"I have a book report."

"OK. Well, do a good job with it."

"Mommy has dinner ready."

"I know. Well, enjoy it. I just wanted to say hi. I miss you. See you next weekend?"

"OK."

"Yup."

"Good. Love you both. Have a good night."

"Love you."

Love ya, Dad."

"Bye."

I hang up and sit down. Everything is spinning and I think that I should reconsider everything. But I know I won't. I'm just scared, that's all.

After a while I feel better and put some soup on the stove. That will be dinner, along with sardines on toast. I make the sandwich and when the soup is hot, I set it down on the table. While it cools I go out for that cigarette I passed on before. The gun is still in my coat pocket. I hold it, and it comforts me.

*　　　*　　　*

I learn a painful lesson tonight. I make the mistake of taking my study notes into the toilet after my coffee. I know better than to stress myself out while I'm trying to crap; I tense up, and can't go without forcing it. That's what happens tonight. I'm sitting for a long time and nothing is happening because I'm too preoccupied with studying, so I start pushing. I'm barely getting anywhere so I push harder, and soon, I can feel my hemorrhoid swelling far beyond its normal size, and blood is running from it, filling the bowl.

"Dammit!"

The toilet is a mess of shit and far more blood than usual. And my ass hurts. I work whatever I can out and try to clean off, but I can't, because the damn thing won't stop bleeding. I stand and blood puddles on the tiled floor. My hands are running with it. And despite lathering ointment all over it, I can't push the hemorrhoid back in. It's too swollen. I am in trouble.

It takes a long time and a lot of blotting with toilet paper to staunch the blood. I clean up the floor and toilet, wash, and gather my notes. But the hemorrhoid is still sticking out of me. It's hard and painful and about the size and shape of a pair of grapes clustered side by side on the vine.

This has happened before, but not in a few years. I thought I had it beat. The damn studying and the damn pushing. I did this to myself for this stupid interview for a job I won't get. It may take a few days before the thing goes down and I can push it back in. And what if it doesn't—that has always been my fear. Go to the hospital and have them cut it off? That would be agony. Plus I don't have any insurance; it would cost me a fortune.

It hurts to walk around, so using as few steps as possible I lay a beach towel across my bed, lay on my stomach over it, and cover my naked ass and legs with another. I have to try and keep my ass elevated so the blood drains away. Then I remember from the last time: ice. I get up and limp to the refrigerator and roll some ice cubes in a dishcloth. I return to the bed and my prone position and fix the ice into my ass crack. Like water on hot coals there is an inaudible hissing, a brutal shock that grips my ass and cuts deep into my colon. And like hot coals, the fire won't quit; it simmers within, and will until the coal burns out completely.

I try to study, but it's hard to focus.

I give up after a while and just lay there, my chin hanging over the edge of the bed, my neck stiff, gazing at the dusty hardwood floor. Despite my misery I have a hardon. But there isn't anything I can do about it. It hurts to move.

Later I force myself up and swallow some Tylenol, chased with a vodka and tonic swallowed in two quick gulps. With each movement, the hemorrhoid seems to swell more. It burns like a cluster of sputtering wires hanging out of my ass. I am very frightened. I don't want to have to go to the hospital. Shaking, I pour and guzzle another vodka.

I take an angry turn once the vodka and the pills hit. I rage and curse like a vengeful wraith trapped in a crippled body. I pitch the rocks glass against the kitchen wall. Remarkably, it doesn't break: the solid glass bottom thuds against the wall, leaving a dent in the plaster, then bounces onto the kitchen table.

I examine the glass. Not even cracked. But I throw it out anyway. I don't want it breaking open in my mouth someday. I stop, and suddenly recall a scene from the movie The Dogs of War. A group of mercenaries, led by Christopher Walken, capture the spy trailing them and proceed to interrogate him. They tie him to a chair and Walken puts the choice to him: tell us who you're working for, and I promise you a quick and painless death. Refuse and you'll suffer. Either way, you're going to tell us, and you're going to die.

The prisoner refuses, and they break a drinking glass in his mouth and work his jaws with their hands to make him swallow it.

As promised, he suffers. And he tells them what they want to know. And then they shoot him.

This gets me thinking. And I'm thinking, we all don't get much of a choice, do we? Nor does anyone even want anything from us. But we all have to bite down on that glass, eventually.

It's all suffering without any meaning.

I load a third round in the gun, lie down on my stomach and try to sleep.

I think of Johanna, and pain.

IV.

I'm awake most of the night worried about the hemorrhoid, and to a lesser extent, the interview. The longest stretch of sleep I get is from four to six. Then the alarm sounds.

Before I move, I gently explore the hemorrhoid with my fingers. It's sensitive, but it isn't outright painful. And it's smaller. But it's still too big to push in and I don't dare try, the pressure would make it swell up more. I spread some ointment on it and consider what to do.

I should stay home from work and lie on my stomach and ice the damn thing all day. That would probably fix it. But I would lose the day's pay. And if something goes wrong with the file job, I would have to go in and fix it.

None of that matters, of course. The ship is going down. Why worry about a day's pay now? And who gives a fuck about the file job? I'm too far gone; I shouldn't be concerned with these things.

But for some reason I cannot fathom, I rise carefully from the bed. And put on the coffee. And fix my breakfast. And go through all the other motions. The only act outside my normal routine is to load the gun in my coat pocket.

And so I find myself at work two hours later, perched like a restless, prancing stork in my chair, trying to keep my weight on one or the other of my hips and off my ass. But it still hurts, and I'm sweating, worried the whole thing will rupture and run with blood. It's happened before.

"You're looking restless today," Ted says.

"It's my back again. I can't get comfortable. It's easier if I stand."

It is. I spend most of the morning on my feet because the pain is getting worse.

The file job is still running fine, and I try to study, but don't make much progress. I limp downstairs a few times with Len for cigarettes, praying all the way. I swallow a few Tylenol. I crap, I can't help it, leaving another bloody mess, and it's very hard to clean myself. I make periodic trips to the toilet to apply ointment. Thank God for the stuff.

I wander around, restless and tired of standing in one place. There isn't much work being done. There isn't much to do. Most people don't have anything to do at all. Some are already packing. Others are throwing out old files. That is their only work.

"You ready for the interview?" Len asks.

"No. I studied, but who knows if I covered what they're looking for."

"This business stinks. I'm completely fed up with technology."

I splurge for a roast beef sandwich from the café in the lobby and eat it standing up in an empty conference room. I skip the after lunch coffee. I assess my swelling and pain objectively. It might be lessening, I think. It's definitely not getting worse. But any sudden movement or a bump in the road while driving—it would be all over.

I cross my fingers.

At a quarter to two I take my notes and go out to my car. I spread the notes on the passenger seat so I can read them. I breathe slow and calm. I've been through this before, and I'm in control. But I'm still nervous. I fondle the revolver. Then at exactly two, I make the call.

The guy doesn't speak English well, and I can barely understand him. I can feel my anger rising, but I force it down. He plays friendly at first, but I can hear an underlying impatience in his tone. I can tell he's mad that I'm not an Indian. The opening banter is minimal, I ask about what kind of project are they working on—because I want know, and also because it might help me answer the questions better if I know what they're looking for. But he won't tell me. First, the interview, he says, loftily. I can tell he thinks he's superior.

Bastard.

He starts firing questions at me. They are Master's level questions, dealing with the underlying structure and functioning of databases. Completely not applicable to the kind of programming I do, and, not anything to be concerned with. It's clearly a set up to make me fail. And I do fail, because I can't answer the questions at all. This is followed by a string of obtuse questions on rarely used programming methods and usages. I can't answer these either, and I ask him: Do you even work with these things? And he says, No, we don't.

I reply belligerently.

"Then why are you asking me about it?"

He's taken aback. He drops the high and mighty attitude and fumbles for a moment. I can't understand what he's saying. Then I deduce that he's telling me they have to interview more candidates and they'll let Bob Smith know if they are interested in me.

"OK," I say, and I hang up.

A harsh click suddenly sounds in my pocket.

I just pulled the trigger of the gun. I'd been squeezing it throughout the entire interview without knowing. The hammer fell on one of the four empty chambers in the cylinder. But it could have fallen on one of the three with a bullet.

I just almost shot myself in the leg.

"Fuck," I say, and begin to shake.

I start the car to crank the window for fresh air. I can feel the panic coming on. I fight back. It takes some time, but for now, I beat it.

My cell phone rings. It's Bob Smith, calling to find out how the interview went. A good recruiter does that. I'm surprised he's doing it. I pick up the call.

"It sucked. Fuck you."

I hang up.

My career in Technology is officially over.

*   *   *

I stop by Len's cube on my way back and lean against its unstable modular wall.

"So how'd it go?"

"Same as the last few times. It was way over my head. And I could barely understand him."

"Fucking bullshit. This field is ruined."

"Well, it moved on while we stayed still."

"Yeah, but is that our fault? Can we help it if we work for a place that never upgrades its technology? We were planning to modernize, you know. This was before you started here. But when the venture capital firm bought the place, they cancelled that. They didn't want to invest any money in the business. They just wanted all the profit and a place to do favors for their friends. Did you know in the first four years after they took over, we had four CEOs? Not one of them knew this business. They were all friends of the venture capital guys. They each took a million plus in salary out of the company and then made way for the next one in line. It was like a revolving door. And not one of them did shit to improve this place. All they did was hack down the budget and hound the sales team to bring in more customers. The sales guys would promise the customers anything to get their business. That's why everything's a mess around here, because we have all these patchwork applications trying to produce what they were never designed to do, to meet all these promises. And we're always jumping through fucking hoops so we don't lose the contracts."

I'm only half-listening. I've heard the story before. My ass is sore. Not painful, really, but raw and worn. The swelling must be going down. I feel anxious, on the verge of panic. Len isn't helping. He goes on and on, working himself up the scale of frenzy. I look down at him at his desk. His eyes are bulging from his reddened face.

"OK, OK," I say. "I know. Calm down."

"Calm down? Why the fuck should I calm down? We're losing our JOBS! Our careers are FINISHED! And this place is to blame, they totally FUCKED us!"

People are passing by, feigning errands, but in fact anxious over Len's outburst. They know him and his ways, and how he and I relate, and I can see they are looking to me to calm him down. That's the way it's always happened before. But I don't feel like playing according to that script. I feel like improvising.

"So what are you going to do about it?" I ask Len.

"What?"

"OK, we got fucked by this company. What are you going to do about it?"

He looks at me strangely.

"What the fuck do you mean? What the fuck can I do?

Quit? I'll lose my severance and I won't get Unemployment. I can't do anything. I'm fucking trapped."

"You're never trapped. There is always a way out."

I'm slipping. I'm getting loud. It's like this dream I often have where I'm sliding down a great, steep slope and can't stop myself. Sometimes I'm on foot, or in a car with failed brakes. It's frightening and exciting at once. I fight to stop myself, but can't. I'm not sure what's at the bottom of the slope; it looks like it might be a busy intersection, a cluster of people and moving vehicles. The worst is a version where I'm in the car, and it's stalled, and I'm rolling backwards down the hill, plummeting into the unknown, because I can't see what's behind me at all.

It feels like that now. And the people are watching me.

"And what's your way out?" Len asks.

My hand is gently squeezing the gun now. Index finger slipping over the trigger. What are the odds? Three out of seven? I can't convert that to a percentage. Maybe Len can. Maybe the president of the company can. Is he upstairs today? Or is he sucking up to the buyers at the home office?

I am in the car, rolling backwards.

I loaded the three bullets next to each other. There are four empty chambers in the cylinder running in sequence. When I pulled the hammer in the car it fell on an empty chamber. If I pull the trigger again, the possibilities are:

One empty chamber…

Two empty chambers…

Three empty chambers…

Or three rounds in sequence.

Bang bang bang.

"This is my way out!" I exclaim, and I pull my hands from

my pockets and slap my crotch. "Porno webcam! I'm gonna jerk off for cash on the internet! Live shows at nine and eleven, five nights a week!"

A bad joke, but it's the first thing I can think of. And it gets my hand off the gun.

The brakes work, this time.

I can see eyes rolling as the gallery of passing faces relax and transform from concern to disgust.

But not Ted's. I see him peering around the corner of the aisle. He's looking at me like he's trying to read a foreign alphabet. Then he disappears.

So do the others. I hear a few remarks as they fade away, such as: "idiots" and "gross".

"You're fucked up, man," Len says and shakes his head. I strung him along and fucked with him, and he fell for it. That's how it looks to him, anyway.

"Let's get a smoke," I say. I really need one.

"Sure," Len says.

Carl is down there smoking, too. Carl is under a lot of pressure. The buyer is breathing down Management's neck, and they breathe down his. He has to rally us to provide what they need. And that changes every day. To his credit, he doesn't take it out on us. Instead he smokes a pack a day. He's fifty pounds overweight, red in the face, and wheezes all the time. He tells us he sleeps only two or three hours a night.

I don't think he'll live much longer.

"How's the file job coming?" he asks.

"Fine," I say. "Probably finish tonight."

"Good. You had an interview today?"

"Yeah, but no go."

Len launches into a rant on my behalf on the Indian Takeover and how they've locked up technology. I don't have to say anything. Of course I don't agree with most of it. But I'm not made of the stuff that scaled Mt. Suribachi, either, so I don't feel like half the victim Len makes me out to be. I've been unemployed, or tentatively employed, for two years now, with bleak prospects, and what have I done to change that? But I honestly don't think there is much I could have done—changing careers was always an option, but that would mean losing half my salary. Which is really the issue for all of us—accepting, in our forties, some of us with homes, most of us with children— starting all over again, and having our standard of living halved. No mean feat when most of us have their incomes tied up in mortgages. Or in my case, overdue bills and child support. Maybe it's unfair, but I still feel like a failure. And I think most everyone else does, too.

Are we losers or not? Is there a way to fix this that we can live with?

I don't fucking know. I'm just sick of thinking about it.

The point is moot. I've chosen my path. And it isn't Len's or Carl's or Ted's or Nanette's.

It's nearly quitting time. Ted is packing his bag when I get back to my cube.

"What's up with you?" he asks without looking up.

"What do you mean?" I grip the arms of my seat and lower myself gently into it, taking care to keep my weight off my ass.

"You're acting really weird this week. Weirder than normal. More like, crazy."

"So, I'm crazy. I've always been crazy."

Now he's staring at me and it's making me uncomfortable. It's making me feel like I've been…caught.

"I think you need to get a grip," he says. "You're slipping."

"It's been a rough week. We got our notice, remember?"

"Yeah, sure, but we knew that was coming a long time. I'm just saying don't let it get the best of you. Whatever is it, just let it pass."

"OK."

"Things will get better. Spring is just around the corner. I'll have the boat on the water soon. I want you to bring your kids down, I'll take them fishing. Kids love to fish. You have to think of them, right?"

"Of course."

"OK. Don't forget. See you tomorrow." He's gone.

I sit and stare at his empty cube. Why did he say all that? Does he know? I was away from my cube a number of times today, and I didn't take my coat. Did he look in the pocket?

And the fishing. I've known him for four years and suddenly he invites me fishing. He's only taken two other guys in the company fishing, two old-timers like himself. Ted's been working here almost thirty years, and the other guys almost as long. Nobody else has gone fishing with Ted. Why me?

Why my kids? I have to think of them, that's what he said. My poor kids. They've never been fishing off a boat. I have to take them fishing in the Spring.

Things will get better, he said. This will pass, he said.

Will it? It's been going on like this for two years, and nothing has changed.

Nothing will change, will it?

I have to be more careful, now. Ted is watching me.

*　　*　　*

When I get home, I want to get drunk. Really drunk. To hell with it that I have work tomorrow. I'm going to get drunk.

But first there are things to do.

There's a voicemail from my mother. I don't call her back. Another from my sister in California. I'm not calling her back, either.

That's done.

I eat hotdogs and salad for dinner. I put mustard and mayonnaise on the dogs. Nobody else I know does this. I don't tell anyone. I always eat my hot dogs alone. The secrets start out small. Eventually they get bigger.

Then coffee and a cigarette and suffering through another hour-long crap. The blood and the swelling and the index finger shoving the hemorrhoid back up the rectum. Twice a day, day after day, for years already. I'm can't stand it anymore. But I don't think anyone could have taken it as long as I have.

At least, I console myself, the swelling went down. It bled itself out, I suppose. I got lucky, again.

I take a shower. It feels good. I pull on a sweater and my "drinking pants"—a pair of jeans torn to shreds. Lacerated knees, cuffs frayed like white lace, and a finger hole in the crotch where the head of my dick pokes through—I don't wear underwear. I have it patched with masking tape inside and out. The inside tape covers the gummy underside of the outer patch, so my dickhead doesn't get stuck to it. I throw on my leather coat, feel the comfort of the gun in the pocket, and step out for a cigarette. The air is icy and smooth and refreshing, like a shot of frozen vodka. My wet hair crackles as crystals of ice form in it. I take long drags on the cigarette and relish a few moments of peace. I'm relaxed, knowing I'll soon be drinking.

I text my friend Gene, ask him to drop by. He's about my only friend anymore. I have others that I see from time to time, but he's the only constant friend I have left. I don't know why the others went away. Or maybe I went away. I'm not sure.

Gene replies. He is coming. I'm glad. He doesn't drink anymore, but it doesn't matter. It doesn't hold me back. And it doesn't bother him. He's done enough drinking of his own to understand.

And that's why he's my only friend anymore, because he understands.

But I don't tell him everything.

I pour vodka, because it's a little party. Vodka and tonic, to start off. My favorite drink. I feel like I've come back to some place I've lost when I taste it. It lightens me up. It makes me sparkle. It feels good. A man has to feel good once in a while. What's wrong with that?

I'm pouring my second when Gene arrives. He knocks, and I yell, "Go away!" like I always do.

Old jokes for old friends.

Gene is my age. We went to high school together. We were only casual friends then, but over time, we've become best friends. He doesn't have anyone else, either. No wife, no woman; our mutual friends all married, and staying married, and not able to get out and drink and shoot the shit on anything like a regular basis.

Gene has drifted through life. In the past few years he decided to get into social work. He's just getting his career off the ground. He's going to graduate school and working part-time. But he's unsure of it all. He can't commit to the profession. He's on his way somewhere, but he's not sure he wants to go there. I, on the other hand, know where I want to be, but I can't get there.

We are just flotsam and jetsam. We joke about it.

"Hey flotsam," I say, as he walks through the door.

"Hey jetsam," he replies.

"How's it hangin?"

"A little to the left."

I smile. I am going to enjoy tonight. I will let nothing spoil this time with Gene. Like nothing should spoil my time with my kids. Some things are pure, and should not be tainted. Our get-togethers are good times for Gene, too. He lives with his widowed mother, who is stubborn, bad-tempered, and won't leave him in peace. He's glad to get a chance to get out and come over to see me every week or so.

Gene puts on water for coffee. When he quit drinking he took up gourmet coffee. He brings his own grounds and brew cup when he comes over. I already have a mug and spoon and the sugar laid out for him.

He has a brown paper bag with him.

"For you," he says. He reaches inside, grasps the neck of the protruding bottle, and strips the bag away and tosses it aside. He's brought a fifth of good tequila.

"Thanks, man. And perfect, I'm running low."

"Yeah, I noticed last week."

"You didn't have to, though."

"Hey man, I come over here all the time and eat up your kids' popcorn and potato chips, so the least I can do is bring something once in a while."

"Cool."

Gene brews his coffee and settles down on the sofa. I ease myself into the big cushioned club chair. My kids call it the "comfy chair." And it is. I got it when I got divorced. They used to fight over who got to sit in it. One Sunday they fought so much I got mad and turned it upside down for the entire afternoon.

"I'll turn it over again when you learn how to take turns," I told them.

They eventually came to an agreement, and I flipped it back.

I raise my glass.

"A toast," I say, "to the official end of my Technology career."

I tell him about the interview.

"That sucks, man," he says. "They all seem to go like that."

"That's the last one," I say, "I give up on Technology."

"Well, you've said that before. But you keep coming back for more. You won't let go, and that's been holding you back."

That's what makes Gene such a good friend. He tells the truth. He doesn't pussyfoot around so as not to hurt your feelings, like everyone else does, nowadays.

"I know. I still haven't let go. I guess because I don't where to go if I do."

I haven't let go of Johanna, either. I'm drinking from a tall glass I got from a bar when we went on vacation at Rehoboth Beach. I have two of these glasses, still; mine and hers. It was a special; buy the Drink of the Day and keep the souvenir glass.

Why do I keep them? Gene is watching me. He knows where the glass came from. But he doesn't say anything about it. I suppose he figures one harsh truth a night is enough.

"Yeah, well, it's not easy letting go of a career, when you don't have an alternative," he says.

"No." But I have an alternative. It's tucked away behind the gin bottle.

"Anyway," I say, "fuck it already. I'm sick of talking about it. Let's talk shop."

That means women. We swap tales of our attempts at getting laid. He's working on some of the grad students. It's a long shot given he's about twice their ages. He talks about them for a while. I mix another drink. I don't have anything to offer to the discussion; after Johanna I went back to internet dating but didn't get far with it. I didn't have the heart for it anymore. The only women I encounter are in bars, but I haven't been out much lately. So I have nothing new to report. Instead I relive a few past glories, replaying a few drunken hookups for Gene's amusement. But I don't have the heart for those either, anymore. When it happens, it's the drinks driving me to do it.

Still, I think if I could only meet some woman and get really messed up in her, I could put Johanna behind me once and for all. And maybe the reason that I haven't is because I don't want to let that happen. I don't ever want to put Johanna behind me once and for all.

I laugh out loud. I have a good buzz on. Gene looks at me.

"What?"

"Never mind," I say. "It's nothing. Private joke between me and myself."

I laugh because I suddenly find it so damn funny how I'm thinking and doing the same things over and over again like nothing has changed. But things have changed. I suppose I'm just a pathetic creature of habit, an organic automaton still going through the motions of normalcy and civilization like a white-collar commuter in the wake of a nuclear holocaust, stepping gingerly over stacks of ruins, feebly trying to make seven-fifteen train to the city. When of course there is no more train, no more station, and no more city. While the more adaptable survivors, the ones with courage, are picking through the rubble for scraps of food and siphoning gas to head for the hills, I'm crying beside the twisted barbs of steel that once conveyed the trains. And the damn thing is, I have in my possession the means to change everything, to stop being the automaton—but do I have the guts to use it?

I wish I could talk to Gene about it, but I can't. I can't talk to anyone about it except for myself.

Another drink. I'm mildly drunk. That good, early-on drunk when it feels like I'm surfing a wave of energy and enthusiasm. I feel like having fun. I feel like I'm having fun. I don't care about my problems. I put on some music.

"Yee hah!"

"What is it?"

"Fuck it all," I say. "I feel good. Fuck it all!"

Gene sure is missing out, because no amount of coffee can make you feel like this.

"I'm free!" I cry, "free! No more Technology. No more nothing!"

"Been a long time coming."

"You got that right, brother." I reached across the coffee table and tap his mug with my glass. A grinning swordfish smiles at me from my glass, the mascot of that bar at Rehoboth Beach.

"You should take up drinking again, man."

"Yeah, I've been thinking about it."

"Better chance of hooking up with your little grad school girls. You need a few drinks for the courage to make an ass out of yourself. Because you're gonna look like an ass going for those young twats. But that's the name of the game, my friend. They like it when you make a fool of yourself, they like the attention. And hey, maybe it will eventually pay off. Listen, better to play the fool for the young honeys rather than the Milfs. You know how I've been chasing after these Milfs for years. All they want is to taken out to dinner—by like three guys a week. You should see their online dating ads—you'd think their twats are made of gold, how perfect they describe themselves. They talk all this shit about wanting adventure, and romance, and a soul mate, but when you take them out it's dinner or nothing, and you better pay, or you're history. It's all about the money with them. Yeah, you know it when they put on their profile that they're looking for a man who's 'secure' or 'established'. Those are the code words."

But what woman in her forties wants to go out with a guy who's broke? Who can't afford to go anywhere or do anything?

Can I really blame them for that?

"Anyway, forget the Milfs, man, what can you offer them? Your career is barely off the ground. And me? Forget it. Just go out and get drunk with the young girls. Or just buy them enough to get them drunk, and just have a few yourself."

"I know. It's just hard to stop once I get started."

That's how Gene was. He'd drink till he dropped. When he smoked, it was two packs a day. There was no in-between. Funny, for such a mellow guy. So now he does nothing. Just coffee. All that caffeine. I wonder, does he sleep at night?

"Well, anyway, just keep casting your net. You'll reel one of them in eventually. Snare yourself something that stinks like fish."

This is really funny to me, and I laugh so hard I hurt my ribs.

"Well, man, I gotta get going," Gene says. "Got an early class."

He gets up quickly, without looking at me. I hope I didn't' piss him off. I always wonder, with me drunk and him sober, did I say something to piss him off? Although it is true, he does have an early class on Friday.

"OK, man. Glad you came."

He gathers his coffee, brewcup, and filters. I give him a hearty slap on the back, and head outside with him for a cigarette. I don't bring a jacket but I don't feel the cold.

He stands with me while I smoke.

"Yeah," he says. "What the fuck."

It feels like he wants to talk about something. Why didn't I notice that before? I feel bad.

"What's up, man?"

"Don't push me to drink. You keep doing that. I've been feeling lately like I want to start up again, and trying to fight it off. I have enough fun without it. I'm fine hanging out when you're drinking, but when you push it on me, it messes me up."

"Man, I'm sorry."

"It's all right. Anyway, I'll catch you soon."

"OK. Take it easy."

He gets in his car and drives off. Something inside of me drops away and vanishes. The sky is black and the cold closes in. The cigarette is no food for my soul; it's a choking stub of ash. I flick it violently into the pile of plowed snow on the curb and hurry inside. I wonder when, or if, I'll see Gene again.

*   *   *

How many drinks have I had? Four? I have to take it easy, I have to go through the motions and go to work tomorrow. I can have two more. Just no more doubles.

The music is too upbeat, so I change the CD. I put on something downbeat and plaintive. Counting Crows. When I feel good, the music drives me. Now I'm driving the music.

I fix a drink and fall into the easy chair, spilling vodka and tonic all over myself and the fabric. It doesn't matter. I've done it before.

I sit and think. Today was my last chance at Technology. And not much chance at that. But I knew that. One more avenue eliminated. I can load another round in the gun, now. I should, before I get so drunk I shoot myself by mistake. Shit, I almost did it today when I was sober.

I add another bullet to the cylinder, in line with the others. Four in a row. Three empty chambers remain.

I jolt awake from a drunken torpor. I spill my drink again. I was in a daze, half passed out. Did an hour pass? The .38 is clutched in my right hand. I panic, thinking I woke up because it went off in my hand. I open the cylinder: four rounds. I shut it and put the gun safely away.

Now all that remains in my hand is the glass from Rehoboth Beach and some unfinished business.

If it were only the glass, maybe it would be OK. But it's not just the glass. It's the girl I saw last month, heading uptown to the bars, rummaging with both hands in her purse under the light of the street lamp, balancing the purse on one upraised leg. Like Johanna did. The girl had the same dark hair, the same curvy figure. But it wasn't Johanna. It's her car I see so often in the parking lot just a few blocks away from my apartment, where she works. It's my compulsion to scan the crowds in the bars, dreading and yearning to see her, even though I know she wouldn't come out when she knows I might be afoot. Or how I know where she is, instinctively; driving her kids to her ex-husband, or coming home from work, or going to bed early on Friday nights; all her comings and goings, and aware of them without being witness to them because I know her habits and her ways, which are immutable.

And then there are the dreams.

And I can guess that she awakens the new lover I suspect she has, on Saturday mornings, the same way she awoke me.

If she says the same things to him on Saturday morning that she said to me, then Love is nothing but a lie, just a another cheap disposable thing, and three years of my life is without meaning.

Compared to that, the bar glass is nothing. I could smash it, grind it into pumice and cast it on the wind but it wouldn't change anything.

I'm sitting in front of my computer, bringing up my email. I don't know what I'm doing, and know what I'm doing, at the same time. And there are hollow shouts of warning echoing in my head: she is impossible, she tried to control you, she tried to bend you to her will with her temper. Yes, all true; I know, but now I'm addressing an email to her. And then I write:

I'm heartbroken

I miss you

I want to be with you again

And then it's gone. I've sent it.

Then something happens that never happens. I pitch forward and vomit. The bile spreads across the floor like an amoeba grown ten-thousand fold and set free to gasp and bubble and die at my feet.

I've done the thing, and now I can't take it back.

Or have I done the thing I should have done long ago?

I vomit again, followed by a spasm of painful heaving. Some fibrous thread, running from my chest to my groin, tears. It hurts worse than my heaving gut and I groan.

I'm not drunk anymore. I'm sick. I lean forward, clutching the table with both hands, my head hung low in defeat. I do that for a while. Then I slowly and painfully clean up my mess.

V.

I am not well in the morning. I stagger around naked in the cold for a while, trying to orient myself, turning on the lights, putting away glasses, fiddling with the coffee maker. I can only stomach coffee and orange juice. Immediately I have diarrhea, which is a blessing, because it cleans me out in half the time I would normally take in the toilet. Afterwards, I log on to my computer to see my email now, instead of waiting to reach my cube at work, dreading what I might find. Nothing.

Everything is upside down.

I slowly shower and dress, secure the gun in my coat pocket, and leave for work. I'm fairly clear-headed by that time. Good enough to drive. I didn't drink enough to really mess myself up, but I came close.

"Carl was just here looking for you," Ted says.

"Shit." When Carl looks for you first thing in the morning, there is trouble.

I find him down in the deck, smoking with Len. The smoke turns my stomach. I hope that passes soon, because I really want a cigarette.

"You look like shit," Len says.

"What's up, Carl?" I say.

"The files are not right," he says, and explains a mistake in calculation I made on one of the modified data fields. And Nanette had questioned how I made that calculation. "You have to fix it and run them all over again. They are very pissed."

Carl is not a bad boss. I fucked up and set the schedule back nearly a week and the buyers and our management certainly gave him a hard time on this, but he doesn't act mad. Instead he shrugs and shakes his head in resignation as if to say, "It's just another day, and just another fuckup by my fucked-up team."

Yes, I'm a fuckup, but I'm the only fuckup you can get to do this job. Nobody else would.

"I'm sorry," I say. "OK, I'll go fix the shit and start it up again." I hurry back upstairs.

I'm losing this job in four weeks and I shouldn't care about this. What does it matter anymore if I made a big mistake? But I do, because I still have to fix it, and I'm going to stress about whether it's going to work the second time.

And I have to present my change to Nanette. My heart is racing and my guts are twisted in protest. I'm mad at myself for being so stupid. I'm going through the motions, but the motions are all too real.

But most of all, I'm dreading confronting Nanette. She never holds back from 'I told you so,' when we make mistakes she flagged in advance. And she will tear apart everything we've done to make sure it's 100% right on the second try.

Making the fix is easy. It takes an hour to put it in and run a test. I put a new submission document together and email it to Nanette. Then, with dread, I head to her office.

But I make an unexpected detour. I suddenly have to throw up. I make it to the men's room just in time. I make a mess on the toilet seat and have to clean it up. I look in the mirror when I'm done. My pale face is twisted in a desperate grimace. There are sickly, gray circles under my eyes.

I wash my face and take a few minutes to calm myself. Then I head over to Nanette's.

"You probably know why I'm here," I say.

"I sure do," she says.

"You were right. Lay it on me."

"Are you sick?"

"No. Why?"

"You look awful. Really pale."

The bleeding is wearing me down. It's happened before. If I don't get it under control soon, I'll turn jaundice yellow. That happened a few years back. I had to have a transfusion, four units of whole blood.

"I feel a cold coming on."

"So what exactly happened?"

I explain my mistake with the calculation.

"I told you about that."

"You did."

"It pays to do things right the first time, you know."

"I know."

"That's my job. I'm not here to make things hard for you guys. I'm here to help you avoid mistakes and problems for yourself."

"I know you are."

"So how did you fix it?"

I explain.

"And you didn't touch anything else?"

"No."

She looks me over.

"I know the files are late. But there's no sense in me getting involved in it now. Just have Carl sign off on it again."

"Thanks, I appreciate that."

I hurry away to find Carl. I got off easy. I suppose she's resigned herself to the fact that it doesn't matter anymore and there's no sense in raking me over the coals. But she's right, of course. I don't always do things right, and I should, despite the pressure to hurry. This is nothing new. But it doesn't really matter; Nanette does things the right way and I do them the wrong way, and we're both losing our jobs.

Carl is smoking again. He will probably go through an extra half-pack today over this. He signs the document. I bring it to the systems guys that actually have to run the job. I go straight to their boss, Rich.

"Sorry, but I gotta ask you guys to run this again. I fucked it up. But I fixed it. The buyer is really pissed, so can you please start it right away?"

"Like I give a fuck if they get their files on time?" booms

Rich. "Fuck those cocksuckers. I'm glad their shit is late and I'm glad you fucked it up for them. If I had a medal, I'd pin it on your chest right now."

He gives me a salute and snatches the document from my hand to give to one of his guys to restart the job.

I go to my cube and sit down. Rich's words ring in my head, and cause me wonder: did I sabotage the job on purpose? Something is not right. I don't have a clear line of thought and action. Nanette pointed out the problem, but I blithely ignored it. The job fails, and I'm in a panic. I'm still acting like it matters anymore. I'm polishing the candelabra in the grand ballroom of the Titanic. Meanwhile, I've brought a gun to work for the third day in a row.

The gun. And Ted. I know he's watching me. I meant to keep my coat on at all times from now on, so he won't find it if he snoops. I check the pocket. It's still there. Ted is engrossed in a game of Tetris. I put the coat on. He turns to me.

"Cold?"

"Yeah, it's cold in here."

Shit, did he look?

"So you fucked up again. You fix it?"

"Yeah, I did."

"What did Nanette say?"

"She let me off easy."

He shakes his head.

"She wants you, baby."

"Oh my god. I wouldn't fuck her with your dick," I say, and shoot a rubber band at him.

He looks at me squarely. "Just give it up," he says.

I'm trying to make fun, but I'm just acting. I'm worried. Ted has barely spoken all day. He merely grunts at my insult. He should have replied with a volley of rubber bands. And then there was his talk of the boat, and my kids, yesterday. He must know.

What did I expect, bringing the damn thing to work with me?

I go outside for a cigarette. I finally feel that I can stomach one. I go far out into the parking lot, to my car, to get away from everyone. I lean against the salt-encrusted quarter panel, facing away from the building. I shiver in the pale winter light.

If Ted really knows, what will he do? Will he get the police? Tell Carl? Or will he try to talk me out of it? Was that what he tried yesterday?

In a fight, you have to give your opponent a way out. If they're trapped, they'll fight harder than if they have an escape. It's like cornering a rat—they'll lunge at your face when they would normally run. With a person, you need to leave them some dignity--you can beat them, but you still have to leave them something. You give them your hand to help them off the ground when you knock them down, instead of kicking them in the ass, or mocking them as they roll off the curb into the gutter. Otherwise they'll keep fighting, or if they can't, they'll come after you later. Maybe I'm the rat, here. Ted may figure a direct confrontation will make me do something crazy. Is he beating around the bush, making a subtle point, and giving me a way out?

"Just give it up," he said before.

I could.

I slide down the side of the car, dragging a thousand crystals of salt with the back of my jacket, scoring the quarter panel with a thousand jagged lines in my wake. I don't stop until my ass comes up hard against the cold ground.

I just want things to be normal again. A job. A woman. My kids close by. A future.

I had all these things once, and now they're gone. How can I get them back?

I look around. Am I expecting an answer? The bleak sky, the barren trees, the rows of dirty cars. All mute, of course.

The heron flies past, along the edge of the far-off tree line, slowly working its long wings. Is that supposed to mean something? It means nothing. What are you still doing here, you stupid bird. There is nothing here for you anymore. Go somewhere else.

I could give it up. Walk to the tree line and pitch the gun into the sterile pond in the woods.

But then I'd have nothing anymore, like that stupid bird.

I don't know. So, I will go through the motions. It's time to go to lunch. I go.

*   *   *

I anxiously check my email after lunch. But there is nothing from Johanna. I know she's read the email by now. And I know she's mad. I have upset her equilibrium. Her answer to that was always anger. Sudden anger; so I am puzzled as to why she hasn't replied. It's not like her to formulate thoughtful responses. More likely she's ignoring me. I shouldn't have sent the email. Just another stupid thing I've done drunk. There's no hope for us anymore.

Although I must believe there is, or I wouldn't have sent it.

The file job is running fine. The files look good. I don't get emails from the buyers, but Carl does, and when I see him at the coffee machine, he tells me he heard from the buyer, and they've received the first batch of the corrected files. I'm sure there's a lot more he heard from them that he doesn't tell me.

"That's why he makes the big bucks," Len says. We're downstairs smoking. "He has to take the shit."

"Yup."

"Hear back from that recruiter?" he asks.

"No, and I don't expect to. You have any irons in the fire?"

"I'm talking to a couple of recruiters, but nothing. I'm spent, man. I'm sick of it all. I don't even want to look for a job anymore. I'm tired of banging my head against a brick wall. I just wanna go home and sleep for a year. Fuck it all."

A few of the Spaniards from the other side of the building come down to smoke. They work for a Spanish company that imports wine, olive oil, and gourmet foods. They're all younger; thirty at the most. The guys are hip, stylish, and the girls are dark, slim, and gorgeous. They're all happy, easygoing, relaxed. I look at them with envy and pangs of remorse. I wish I were them.

They're friendly, too, although the girls don't say much. Len and I talk to the guys often, and sometimes, to the girls. But the girls aren't very interested. We're pushing fifty; although, if I have anything going for me, it's that I'm in great shape, have all my hair and could pass for ten years younger than I am. I've lied to women in bars about my age and never been questioned. I tell them I'm forty, a claim plausible enough not to cast suspicion. But these girls are in their late twenties at most. And this is the middle of the day and they're sober.

Len, however, always tries to chat them up. I don't think he's on the make; he's just looking for some attention. He starts on the guys, telling them about our layoff, our trouble finding jobs, and expands his circle of engagement to include the girls. I'd like to tell him that airing our miseries isn't going to impress the girls or get us laid. I just play a distant wingman and nod. I don't feel like airing my misery. The girls don't say much in response. But the guys talk to us. They're shocked to hear how low the Unemployment benefits are.

"In Europe when you lose the job, you get the rent paid by the government. And the heat and electricity. And you get money also; not all your job money, but something. You don't need much because they pay for the apartment. They pay for years."

The thought of laying unemployed and carefree all day on the beach at Barcelona with dark Spanish women passing in an endless topless rhythm, and the boardwalk cafes with their cheap, strong wine, is maddening. My soul is blue-balled with the utter unattainability of it.

"Well this is America and we don't even get half our salary and nothing else. And you get cut off in two years. Then you're fucked up the ass!" Len exclaims.

The Spanish guys like Len. He's very colorful. But the girls are visibly turned off.

"Well, it is still bad in Spain. We have very many people without work. Taxes are very high, to pay for helping them. But we have to."

I find myself staring at one of the girls. She's beautiful. She reminds me of Penelope Cruz if bit more curvaceous. She notices my stare, and gives me a thin, uncomfortable smile. I feel bad—I'm just another leering older guy with eyes crawling all over her body. I look away. I want to apologize to her. Not as a joke, or as a sly means of picking her up. I really want to apologize.

I laugh to myself, because I'd really like to fuck her, too. Then I'm unnerved. Everything in my head, I realize, is backwards, contradictory, and confused. My thoughts and feelings aren't staying put in one place anymore. Not even for a second. All the joints in my brain are dislocated. My body feels fine, but my mind feels drunk. Like it's staggering home along the sidewalk after closing time.

I need to gather my wits—what an apt expression. Yes, I can see it perfectly; I have to form two great arcs with my arms and gather my scattered thoughts and feelings into a tight pile and put them back together. Like scooping up a shattered Humvee after a roadside bomb blast on a Baghdad side street.

And I need my wits on hand—another apt way to put it, on hand—because I have something important to do, and I need to do it soon.

"Hey, guys," I say to the Spaniards, interrupting Len's monologue. He shoots me an annoyed look. "Do you know this American expression?"

"What expression?"

"I gotta get my shit together?"

"I think. What does it mean?"

"It means, 'I have to get organized.'"

"Oh yes. I have heard it from the American guys in the office."

"Yup. Have you seen *Taxi Driver*?"

"No," the Spaniard says. Len is looking at me, puzzled.

"I do," Penelope Cruz says. I'm surprised. "Robert DeNiro; he killed the pimp and rescued the girl in the brothel."

"Yes, that's right. Great movie. Well, the guy, the taxi driver, he had a poster in his room, it said, 'I gotta get ORGANIZIZED.'"

"So?" Len says.

"It was a joke—it's misspelled. It should be 'ORGANIZED'. But it's important for the movie, because the guy took a long time preparing himself for what he had to do—he killed the pimp in the end, but he was really trying to kill a political candidate. He's trying to get his shit together."

"OK," says Spanish guy.

"So what is your point?" Len says.

"The point is, I gotta get my shit together. I gotta get organizized."

The Spaniards politely chuckle, as if I made a joke they don't understand but want to acknowledge my generous effort to share it with them.

Len responds differently.

"What the fuck are you talking about, man?"

"You ever see the movie?"

"No."

"Then you're more culturally deficient than I imagined. In fact our whole company is, not to mention this entire country. Look, this girl here, from Spain, half your age, saw this very important movie. Probably in English, which is not her native language. And in Spain, and the rest of Europe, they care about their unfortunates. They are advanced culturally, linguistically, and politically. But here, here, we're still in the Dark Ages."

The Spaniards are puzzled. But Len is pissed.

"I still don't get it. So what the fuck are you saying, you're going to assassinate somebody?"

"No, only important public figures can be assassinated."

"You lost me, man. I don't know what the fuck you're talking about, but I do know you got a screw loose."

Len doesn't know anything. I like fucking with him when he goes on stage and tries to grab the spotlight. But for all that light, he ain't too bright.

The Spanish guys mutter farewells and wish us a good weekend and drift back into the building. And as she passes through the door, Penelope glances back at me and gives me a look of concern. I wish I had had a chance to talk to her some time. She has such knowing, beautiful eyes. If I could spend a night just staring into those eyes up close, I would forget a lot of things I ought to forget. But she's as far away as Barcelona.

No, that's not it.

I'm too far away.

*   *   *

Back at my cube, the job is running fine. And still nothing from Johanna. If I haven't heard from her by now, I don't think I will.

Or maybe, since she's at work, she doesn't want to get into it while she's busy. Maybe I'll hear from her later, once she's back from dropping her kids with their father for the weekend like she does every Friday.

Friday. I'm getting drunk tonight, I know it already. I'm not sure where and I don't know with whom, but I'm sure it will be in my apartment by myself. That's how it usually happens.

I'm keeping my coat on. Ted isn't saying much. But I'm sure he's watching me. And I'm watching him, and the clock.

At three-thirty he painfully stands.

"I'm leaving early.   Got an appointment with the chiropractor, this damn sciatica is acting up on me."

"Yeah, sure," I say. "You'll never go anywhere in this company leaving early on a Friday."

He grins and wings me in the ear with a rubber band. I reply with one, two, three, all misses. The third would have hit, but Ted foils that with a slight lean to the left.

"You suck," he says. "You couldn't hit the side of a barn if your life depended on it."

Is he fucking with me? Why?

"If my life depended on it, I'd hit it."

"Sure. You better practice, then."

The sonofabitch knows. And now he's taunting me. No, he's challenging me. He wants me to do something. What? He may know what I have, but what does he think I'm going to do with it? He can't know that, he can't get in my mind.

I want to ask him, but when I look up, he's gone.

I'm not worried about him now; if he wanted to get me in trouble he could have long ago. I'm just really puzzled. I try to make sense of what he's doing. First, he let me know he was on to me. Then he seemed to warn me away from it. But now, it sounds like he's not only all for my walking around with a gun in my pocket, he's challenging me to do something with it.

Does he think he's my accomplice now? If he does, then he doesn't understand what's going on at all. He only thinks he does. I'm not doing anything for him, or anybody else. This is all for me.

The last half hour drags. It's so quiet I become aware of my breathing, and when that happens, it ceases to be an involuntary function. Then I have regulate it consciously, but I can't, and I nearly hyperventilate. This goes on until Len drops by to wish me a good weekend. Gasping, I reply in kind, and finally forget about the breathing. It's four o'clock now. I take a brief glance at my file job. It's fine. I check my email. Nothing. When I stand to go, Rich sees me, and calls across the tops of several rows of cubes.

"Hey, if your job crashes this weekend, we're gonna call you."

"It won't."

"Sure, that'll be a first."

I don't think it will. And I don't really care if it does.

I'm out of here.

As I head outside into the cold, I feel the ghost of the old excitement I used to feel on Friday afternoons at quitting time, when I would have a date, or be meeting friends for sushi and drinks, or seeing Johanna. All the yearning, the promise, the potential of the night. That's all gone now, but I smile at the faint memory.

In the car I decide to get some sushi and bring it home. I'll charge it; I have one credit card I can still use.

*   *   *

I have a hard time at the sushi bar. It's the place Johanna and I used to get our sushi, a hole-in the wall with half a dozen tables, rarely occupied. Sometimes we'd eat there, but usually we'd take it home. They have the best sushi for the best price in this overpriced town. But I realize I should have gone someplace else when Johanna's car pulls up and parks just outside. I'm seized with panic and confusion; how could she be here, it's too early; she should be on the road taking her kids to her ex. There's no way she could be back so soon. I frantically think: is it a school holiday, someone's birthday, is there some reason she'd be here now when she shouldn't be? And there's nowhere to run unless I want to sprint out back through the kitchen where they cook the rice and the Miso soup. And what would the owners think? The woman is already bagging up my order.

Then I realize I could hide in the bathroom. I poise, ready to dash.

But it's not Johanna. It's a guy, about my age, and he heads into the bar next door. Same car, same color, though. This has happened before.

And then I think: is that her boyfriend, driving her car? Does she have a boyfriend? I saw a guy driving her car on my way to work a few months back. It was really her car that time; I saw the plates. It was a bald guy, heading into the morning sun, fiddling with the visor and the seat, adjusting them to his height and reach. His first time behind the wheel of her car. Who would be driving her car a quarter-to-eight in the morning? A mechanic, checking out a problem? I know where she gets her car serviced, I know the guys, and that wasn't one of them. Who else, a friend? She would never lend her car out to a friend, she's too uptight about her things, especially her car.

Unless it was a special friend.

The Japanese woman is asking for payment, and I spill my wallet on the counter. I rummage through my half-dozen credit cards looking for the right one. I should cut the other ones up, or at least put them away, they're a waste of space and confusing. Later. I find the right card and she swipes it but it fails. Wasn't that the one that should work? I try another. It fails. The woman, normally so friendly, is obviously annoyed.

"Do you have card that will work?"

So much for the inscrutable Oriental of lore.

I have to give her my bank debit card, although I don't want to. I want to hold on to the money in my checking account for gas, cigarettes, and liquor. But I have no choice. She snatches the card from my hand. I feel like telling her to lighten up and fuck off and keep her damn sushi. I didn't sit at the bar and eat it yet; she can still sell it to the next guy. It's only four-thirty in the afternoon and I'm sure somebody is going to want a Dragon Roll and Spicy Tuna in the next six hours. I didn't order Sea Urchin or some other exotic shit that no one else eats.

The charge goes through and she hands my card back without a word. I take my bag and squeeze between the rows of tables to leave. The sushi chef, however, looks up from his sharp knife and his salmon to smile and call out, "Enjoy!"

"I will, thanks."

I check the plates on the car outside. They're not Johanna's. I didn't think so; the guy didn't look like the guy I saw the other month. Not that she couldn't have ditched that guy and have a new boyfriend by now. But I know her well and if she let a guy drive her car she has to feel deeply and trust wholly, neither of which come easy nor quick for her. And here's the irony: she was the one that said it would take forever for her to want to be with someone else again. I guess all that talk was just bullshit because just a few months after me, some new guy is driving her car.

I hope it was a mechanic.

There is a lot of activity back at my building. The place hums with anticipation and sexual tension. There are six apartments in my building; they all open to the parking lot in front. There's a yard and a gazebo that only my kids use. Except for me and the old drunk guy, the rest of the apartments are occupied by twenty-something kids. The girls next to me, two dudes on the corner, and two sets of young couples. They all like to drink and party. I've gone out drinking with the dudes, and

I've hung out with the couples. The single girls are apparently too good for me, though. When I pull in the lot, the dudes are coming in with some other guys and a few cases of beer. One of the couples is heading out, hurrying uptown, probably to Happy Hour at a bar or club. And the girls are just stepping out of their car, chatting excitedly and carrying an assortment of shopping bags from the mall. My heart quickens with longing and loneliness.

"Wassup, man?" cries one of the Dudes.

"Not much, how 'bout you guys?"

He hoists the case of beer in his arms.

"Friday, man. Drop in for some beers. We're gonna knock these off and head uptown after."

"Thanks, maybe. If not, maybe I'll see you uptown."

"Cool."

They're good guys. They always invite me when they have parties. I wonder if they would if they knew I'm old enough to be their father. They think I'm in my thirties. And I should go over there. But I don't feel like it. But maybe I should go uptown later. All this excitement is contagious. I haven't been out in a long time.

The sushi and the side of edamame look good. I have my own sushi set, and I set the sushi on the platter, with my own chopsticks alongside. I mix the soy sauce and wasabi in the dipping bowl with the chopsticks. I drop the edamame in the soup bowl.

Johanna gave me this set, and like the bar glasses, I should get rid of it, too.

And the sushi is good. But it's all ruined once I see the email.

Johanna did reply, and just at this very moment. I look at the clock—she's just now home from dropping off her kids. She needed a clear mental field, I suppose. She cannot multi-task with her emotions and never could.

I suspect that I am the opposite in that regard.

"I'm surprised to hear this from you," she has written, "after all this time. After pushing me away for months. And after hurting me like you did, how do you expect me to respond?"

If this were in ink it would still be wet. I can see her in her house. She has just slammed the laptop shut and is storming out of the bedroom.

I'm too stunned to move. But my mind is racing ahead, performing a live autopsy on her words.

Of course she is surprised at what I said, because I did push her away. When I moved out, she said it was completely over. But no sooner was I gone than she wanted to see me. But I was done with her. And I was glad to be gone. I refused her offers to get together. I made curt replies to her texts. She gave up. A month of silence passed. Then, a shift in the paradigm: every few weeks, she would send me a text, just checking in. I replied with terse civility. And so it's been, for almost a year.

So she's shocked to hear I want her again. And I'm shocked, too, because I was right to push her away and keep her away. Why do I still want her? She was eating me alive. And she still is, from within. I can't stop her, and I can't stop myself.

I get up. I dump the sushi and the edamame and the plate and bowl and chopsticks in the trash. Dinner is over. Time for drinking, and no more of this gin or vodka. I fill half a highball glass with tequila and top it off with Coke and a long squeeze of lime. No shots yet--for now I want to take it slow.

And I did hurt her. And I feel a rising fury that she still hasn't gotten over that. One drunken, stupid thing compared to all the shit she gave me. And the unforgiving hell she put me through for it. But I should be grateful for that, because the pain she couldn't overcome was what finally drove her to throw me out. If not for what I did, I might never have gotten free of her. There had to be some insurmountable wedge driven between us to put an end to the whole sorry affair. And my fucking a twenty-eight year old chick I hooked up with in a bar did the trick.

My first drink is already done. I pour another. I'm trying to blot this whole thing out, to stop it before I lose control of it. I should just write her back now, tell her to just forget about it, to delete my email, and goodbye. But I'm going to go on with this, because like I've said, and like I know: I love her as much as I hate her.

*　　*　　*

It was a Friday night in June, almost two years ago. Johanna broke up with me that night. We'd been living together for over six months, and by the third, I knew it wasn't going to work. From the beginning she couldn't deal with me and my kids being there on the weekends. She was openly hostile; storming around, slamming doors and cabinets, not answering when my kids greeted her. It was supposed to be my house too, but I didn't feel welcome in it. And it wasn't good for my kids. She needed her space too much, she had to be in control, and with us around she had neither. And while I could understand it wasn't easy for her to adjust, I couldn't cut her any slack for not controlling her temper. I had to adjust, too, to her kids being underfoot five days of the week. But I wasn't slamming kitchen cabinets or ignoring them. I tried to talk to her about it a few times, but she flipped out. I soon gave up. Maybe too soon. Then I began to withdraw. Both were possibly mistakes.

But I didn't start the shit.

I lost my job at the end of March. Just when I was thinking, maybe I should leave. I thought maybe we can salvage something out of this—still be together, but just live apart. But I couldn't bring myself to do it, there were four kids who would be heartbroken, and two sets of parents, and it was too soon. And then, without a job, where could I go? They don't rent apartments to unemployed people. Later she would accuse me of staying and taking advantage of her because I didn't have a job, but it hadn't come to that yet, in June. I still had some money in the bank and I was paying my way.

No, it was the email that made her break up with me that June night. A week before, I was sitting up late, having some drinks and emailing some friends. I was by then fed up with Johanna and very pissed and I sent a long, half-drunk diatribe to Jack, a long-distance buddy, ripping Johanna to shreds. I told him the whole story, how I was tired of her shit, and closed with some macho "who needs her, I can get another woman anytime" crap. Then I fell asleep on the sofa. And while I was asleep, she came out of the bedroom and read the email. It wasn't accidental; I had sent it, she'd gone into the Sent box to find it.

She never told me this until months later, at our final breakup. Because she knew it was wrong. She could have confronted me right away, but instead she let it burn her up all week. Her hostility was obvious, and she was barely talking, so I asked her what was wrong but she wouldn't tell me. Then on Friday night, she was calmer, and she said, "We need to talk."

She wanted to break up. She was very amicable. It would be just like a divorce. We would split up our joint bank account.

The house was hers, of course; it was in her name. My bad credit had kept me off the mortgage. I remembered all the times she had said, "that doesn't matter, it's your house too," but I didn't bring it up. I didn't have any legal recourse, anyway, which she confirmed by telling me she'd talked to her lawyer about it. I thought that was a little calculated, and over time, the notion that she saw a lawyer came to infuriate me. But that night I was just relieved. It was a good breakup. It was clear she wanted to stay together after I moved out. I wasn't sure about that. And then she said something funny, remarking that if we were seeing other people, we should keep it private.

"I'm not seeing anybody else," I said. Of course I didn't know she'd read my email then.

It was a beautiful, warm night, out there on the back deck with her. A good night to let the past be gone and move on. A good night to forgive and forget. And a great night for some fun.

I suggested we go uptown for some drinks. I had been going out lately, by myself; she wouldn't come with me. In hindsight I suppose she assumed I was seeing some other woman, but I wasn't.

I tried hard to get her to come out; I wanted to have some fun with her, we hadn't done anything together in weeks, we just broke up but there was hope for the future, the tension was broken, let's celebrate. But she just wouldn't budge.

Fate was playing its hand.

So I went uptown alone. It was a long walk, and by the time I reached the Strip, I didn't feel good anymore. I wasn't happy about getting tossed from what was supposed to be my house. I hadn't put much money in it, but I spent what I could spare. And I did a lot of work to fix it up. And now it would be all hers.

And I was frustrated with her, because she just couldn't bend her routine: Friday night, sit at home, watch TV or movies. She just couldn't go out with me, could she? Too set in her ways to come out with me and have a little fun.

I could have stayed home. But I didn't want to. I think I was defying her before I even knew I was mad at her.

I hit a few bars and had a few drinks. I ran into a few people I knew and did a few shots. They drifted off after a while. Somewhat drunk, I wandered outside into the warm night air. The street was crawling with hot, young bodies. The Strip at night, especially in the summer, makes your blood rush. It was the first hot night after a long winter and a cold spring, and it was alive with lust, energy, and possibilities.

Much like a loaded gun.

I wandered around, feeding on the energy. Knowing even if Johanna and I quit for good, there were alternatives. I could just head uptown on a hot summer's night and reach out my hand and grab it.

Satisfied with those thoughts, I began making my way home. I stopped for a cigarette outside the wildest club in town. I felt like watching the girls for a few moments longer. I slung my arm over a parking meter, smoking, while schools of tight little asses, long legs in heels, and surging bosoms flitted past on drunken, incoherent missions.

A skinny blond in glasses burst from the club doorway, turned, locked eyes with mine, and made straight for me.

"Hey, can I have a cigarette," she panted. She swayed bejeweled with glistening sweat in the streetlight's reflection.

She was really cute. Her glasses were slim and hip and worked well on her. She looked like a hot librarian or grad student. Her wild blond hair bounced just above her shoulders.

She was skinny and flat-chested, but she still had a great shape, nice legs, and a tight round ass, gripped in black faux-velvet Lycra.

And she had the most stunning green eyes.

"Sure," I said. "Take two."

We smoked and talked some nonsense I don't completely remember. She was from out of state, she was a makeup artist, and she was out by herself. She was twenty-eight.

"How old are you," she asked. First moment of truth.

I told her I was thirty-eight and she didn't question it.

"You like to dance?" she said.

I hesitated. I remember wondering why I always have such a hard time making the first move. But I hadn't needed to; this girl was so eager.

"Hell yes, let's go." I took her hand and led her back into the club and downstairs to the dance floor. At last, I am bold.

The scene was just shy of a barely constrained orgy and brawl. This was typical of the place, which attracted all the crazies. I'd nearly gotten in several fights there. I had to rescue Gene once, when he was still drinking, from the reach of a guy about to hit him over a girl. He didn't even know it. But I saw the guy cocking his fist, wedged myself between them, and told the guy, "I got it, dude," and grabbed Gene by the collar and dragged him away.

Men in their forties don't belong in this place after eleven. It isn't safe.

"Hey, what's your name?" I shouted.

"Melissa," she screamed.

"What are you drinking?"

"Jack and Coke."

I squeezed up to the bar and got her Jack and Coke and a vodka tonic for me. We took a few slugs and then stepped away from the bar and into the free-for-all on the dance floor. Right away we started grinding. I put my free hand on her ass and pulled her up against my crotch. She moved like a cobra against me.

She reached in her cup and pinched an ice cube between her finger and thumb. She rubbed it all over my chest, around my nipples, and down my shirt.

I may be a slow starter and hesitant around women at first, but once I'm sure, and I'm drunk, I exceed expectations. I took an ice cube of my own drink and explored her open back, mixing the melting cube with her sweat. The cube quickly evaporated on her hot skin, so I took another and slid it down her pants and in her ass crack, rubbing it up and down until it too was gone.

Her response was to swallow her drink in one quick gulp, toss the glass over her shoulder, jam both her hands down my crotch and play with what she found there.

We were soon twirling around the dance floor, our hands down each other's pants, fingering each other, slamming our hips together, and me, working my face down her top, trying to reach her nipples with my tongue. I looked up from Melissa's bosom, slick with sweat and my saliva, and saw a spinning gallery of onlookers, gawking at our exceptional spectacle in a place long-jaded by spectacle.

I stopped and looked at her.

"Let's get out of here," I shouted and emptied my glass, spilling most of it down my shirt.

She nodded, laughed, and began licking the vodka from my chest. I pulled her out of there as fast as I could weave between the grinding sluts, roaring drunks, shot-girls and bouncers.

It was hot outside and the air was fresh. I gasped for breath, and worried that I shouldn't have had that last drink. I wasn't worried that I was going to do something I shouldn't; I knew what I was going to do with Melissa. I was just worried I wouldn't be able to do it.

"Where's your place?" she implored, grabbing my shirt with both hands and shaking me. "Do you have an apartment close? Let's go there, now!"

"Too far, too far," I said. "Where's your car?"

"Down there!" She pointed across the street to the town's brand new parking garage. Her car was on the basement level. We hurried down the ramp. Her little car was just inside, all alone except for a light pickup truck three spaces beyond it.

We jumped inside, she in the driver's seat and I in the passenger's. She keyed on the power and turned on the radio. The station played some mellow jazzy stuff. I was surprised. I expected hip-hop or rap or some other crap.

We began kissing and groping, fumbling awkwardly over the center console, bumping the controls, knocking the wipers on, sounding the horn, and flipping on the headlights.

"When I was a kid we had a car with a bench seat in front instead of this bucket seat shit," I said, and instantly regretted it. It made me sound old.

"Where's that car when you need it?" she whispered.

She pushed me down into the seat and began undoing my pants.

"Wait," I said. "I don't know if I can do this."

"What's wrong?"

"I'm living with a girl. We were supposed to get married. But we just broke up. Just tonight."

That's it, I thought. I'm not getting laid. But I shouldn't—

I'm still living with Johanna, even if she broke up with me. She still loves me. And I still love her, don't I?

"It's OK. Everybody is in some kind of situation. I was in something like that for a while, sleeping on the couch for months until I moved out."

She kept pulling on my cock. It felt so good.

I shouldn't. Johanna. But we did break up tonight. It's over then, isn't it? Let it be, then, let it be over and done.

"OK," I said, and relaxed, and let her go down on me.

I reached around to adjust the seat and she stopped me.

"Don't do that. If the seat isn't just right, somebody is going to want to know who was in the car with me."

So Melissa had a boyfriend. So of course she's not concerned about my personal life. She just wants to get her freak on. I left the seat alone and tried to stop thinking about all these things, because it was too much.

I rarely cum from getting head, no matter how good it is. And she was good. It made me suddenly crazy to fuck her.

"That's enough, girl; lay back, you're getting it, now!" I jumped up and shoved her in the back seat. She giggled crazily.

I was a maniac back there. I sucked and bit her tiny tits, played improvisational jazz with her clit and shoved two fingers up her ass. She drove me crazy like I hadn't been crazy in a long time, if ever. Except for the lack of tits, she had the hottest body, and a perfect ass. I was all over her, and when she started begging, I was in her, fucking her like a condemned man fighting for a reprieve. No, not fucking her—I was beating her, from the inside, brutalizing her, like I'd never done before.

"Oh god I love what you do with your cock!" was all she said, over and over.

I was fucking for my life, in that backseat, fighting all the humiliation, the despair, the misery pent up over four and a half decades, pounding away at the pussy of a girl young enough to be my child, fighting the layoff, the bankruptcy, the cuckoldry of my marriage and the divorce, the awful failing with Johanna—fighting to find who I was and where I left me behind and when; for the unfinished novel and stories packed in an old box in the cellar, for dreams and hopes all dashed to shit on the rocks of my crap-ass life; against the inexorable creep of time, against the age of fifty, just around the corner, and the wasting of my body, my soul long gone; against the virility I would someday lose, that I was losing now, because I'd drank too fucking much and as hard as I was pounding and as good as it felt, my cock was beginning to wither.

"Turn over!" I cried, and without waiting for her to move, I flipped her, and she obliged, poising her ass in a coy, inviting angle.

It's now or never, I thought, before I lose it.

But it turned out to be never.

With spit and the shoe-horning of my fingers I tried to work my way into her ass, but I couldn't make it. My dick was blunted and turned at her tight hole; you need a spear for that, but all I had was a bent truncheon. I had to give it up and settle for just getting back inside her pussy before I lost it for good. I was pissed because her moans and gyrations showed she wanted me in her ass as bad as I did. But I just couldn't make it happen. I slapped my truncheon against her cheeks to bring it back to life and shoved it back in her second-best. I banged away for a while longer, but I soon felt tired and sick and done. I pulled out and fell back. I think she came. But I never did.

Another failure.

Then I heard an engine running, close by. I turned. There

was the pickup truck from before, engine running, and a young guy was sitting in it, looking down at us and grinning.

"Get the fuck out of here, asshole;" I yelled, "show's over." I gave him the finger. He obliged and drove off. Melissa lay on her back, laughing.

"You won't think it's funny when he puts this up on the internet tomorrow."

"He was watching the whole time but he didn't take any pictures."

"What? You could have said something."

"I don't care if anyone watches."

"You're one freaky chick."

"And you really know how to freak out with that big cock of yours." She pulled me down and kissed me long and hard, circling her tongue around mine the way she licked the head of my dick. She tasted like Jack Daniel's and cigarettes. She stroked my limp dick. With a pang of sorrow I remembered all the times I'd come back to a girl for seconds. But not tonight. I was finished.

Fuck it. I fished around the front seat for my pants and pulled them on.

"I should get going," she said. "You need a ride home?"

"Yeah, thanks. But let's exchange numbers. Maybe we can get together again sometime?"

"Sure, you can have my number, I guess."

Why did I feel a pang of broken-heartedness at that? She was just some chick looking to get laid. I was the lucky guy. Be realistic, be satisfied, and let it go. And what about Johanna?

Johanna broke up with me, but she still wanted me.

But what did I want?

Then Melissa turned the key and her car wouldn't start.

"Shit." She tried again. And again. Nothing.

"I shouldn't have left the radio on."

"I could walk the two miles home and get my car and come get you, but I'm too drunk to drive," I said.

"That's sweet. I'll just call AAA."

AAA told her it was a ninety minute wait.

"Why don't you go, you don't have to wait," she said.

"I can't leave you down here alone. It's after closing, there's no place for you to hang out that's safe."

"I'll be okay, you don't have to guard me."

"No, I couldn't leave you alone. Fuck AAA, maybe we can find somebody to jump you. Let's go up to the street."

But the street was deserted. The bars were closed and the crowds long gone. The silence and the stillness were unnerving. The wind had picked up, a warm, damp breath, herding empty cigarette packs and gum wrappers down the sidewalk. Empty bottles clattered along the curb. The supercharge was gone now; the atmosphere was a vacuum, and anything could fill it, good, or bad. I was scared.

A car came down the street, slowly. I waved it down. The driver, a guy in his thirties, rolled down the window. He looked us over, sizing us up. What was he out looking for, I wondered? A lone girl staggering home drunk to rape? A boy? Or just anyone he could roll for their wallet?

"You got jumper cables? My friend's car won't start."

He stared hard at Melissa. I was glad I hadn't left her alone.

"No man, sorry." He sped off.

In the next twenty minutes I saw the same guy, twice, cruising past slowly on the intersecting street. Melissa called

AAA again, but they couldn't promise anything sooner. We sat on the curb and smoked my cigarettes and waited.

Another car came down the street, a girl behind the wheel. I tried to wave her down but she wouldn't stop. She looked drunk and swerved and nearly hit me. I had to jump out of the way.

"Fuck," I cried.

Then a car nosed slowly from the narrow drive alongside the club where we'd danced. It scraped the wall as it emerged into the street. I blocked it, and it stopped. The girl behind the wheel looked panicked until Melissa came up beside me.

"Hey, can you help us? We need a jump start."

I recognized the girl. She was one of the bartenders at the club. A really hot girl, but with a wasted look about her. And her car was a wreck, inside and out.

"What?"

"My friend needs a jump start. She ran down her battery."

The girl looked us over. Then she smiled slightly. Maybe she recognized us. Or maybe we looked too fucked up to be dangerous.

"Sure, where's your car?"

Or maybe she just didn't care about taking risks. She gave me a funny look that made me think that if I were out there alone and needed help, she would help me, and probably fuck me, too. She looked lonely and willing, whether she was going home to someone or not.

Or maybe I was just drunk and thinking I could fuck any young girl now.

She had jumper cables, and Melissa's car started right up. I offered her a few dollars but she refused them. Then she disappeared, swallowed up in the dark streets.

"She was cute," Melissa said. "We should have had a threesome with her."

"You should have suggested that when she was still here."

My cell phone rang. It was Johanna, of course.

"Fuck! It's my girlfriend."

"What are you worried about? You said she broke up with you."

"She did, but fuck! Just be quiet so I can talk to her."

I didn't know what I should say.

"Are you okay?" Johanna said. "I woke up and you're not here and I realized the bars closed two hours ago. Where are you?" She sounded like she was crying.

"I'm okay," I said. Then I gave her a half-lie. A half-lie isn't so bad, I reasoned. I told her I had been with a guy we both knew, and wound up just hanging with a girl friend of his and her car wouldn't start, "and I didn't want to leave her alone waiting for AAA to come and jump her car…"

"You fucking hooked up with some bitch already, just like you meant to, didn't you?" she screamed, and hung up on me.

I didn't understand what she meant about my meaning to hook up already, but I didn't know she had read my email to Jack. What was pure chance to me was premeditated to her.

I felt sick.

"Oh, man, I fucked up," I moaned and buried my face in my hands. When I looked up, Melissa was looking down at me without pity. There would be nothing more with her, I knew; no more big stud. I was pathetic.

"Fuck her," she said. "She broke up with you, didn't she?"

"Yup. But it's not that cut and dry."

"Whatever. You want a ride home?"

"Sure."

I had Melissa drop me off two blocks away, where she could turn around easily, and we wouldn't be seen by Johanna, who was surely watching for me at the window. I was exhausted and completely drunk and made another play for Melissa, insisting we should get together again, knowing damn well she was done with me.

"Maybe," was all she would say, just so she wouldn't have to say No. Nobody likes to say No unless they have no choice.

Melissa sped off and I stumbled the two blocks home. I was passing out on my feet and barely made it. Johanna had put the chain on the door out of spite and I had to call her. She stormed across the living room to unlatch it, pounding the hardwood floor with her bare feet, then stomped, cursing, back to the bedroom. I fumbled through the darkness to the bathroom to piss, then stripped right there and felt my way into bed. I pulled the cover, with the scratchy raised baroque pattern, up to my naked chin. Johanna lay with her back to me.

"Did you fuck her?" she spat.

"No, I didn't fuck anybody. I need to sleep now."

And then I passed out.

*   *   *

Johanna was on me the moment I awoke.

"Tell me the truth, did you fuck that girl?"

"Yes," I sighed.

She leapt from the bed.

"You son of a bitch!" she cried, her face fluid with rage and tears. "You couldn't wait!"

She tore off her sleep sweats and began stuffing her limbs in a fresh gym outfit, fumbling and confusing legs and arms.

"I'm sorry!" I cried. "I was drunk!"

"Fuck you, how long have you been seeing her?"

"It was just a fucking hookup. I never saw her before."

"You're full of shit. I have to get away from you!" She grabbed her purse and her keys and ran from the house.

"Johanna, come back, I'm sorry!"

Her car raced, squealed, and roared away. It was Saturday, eight AM.

I was still drunk, and sick. I ran to the bathroom and threw up until my guts were empty, nearly torn from my throat. But my heart felt worse—like it had been butterflied by an axe. I pulled on some clothes and crawled onto the living room sofa. What the fuck had I done?

An hour later I called Jack.

"It sounds like you broke up with her last night, but she didn't really break up with you. You don't want to be with her anymore, anyway. And from what you've told me, I don't think you should. So stop feeling so bad and roll with it. Hang tough, man."

But I didn't. I twisted and turned on the sofa, suffocating on regret, choking on shame for ruining everything and heartsick for hurting Johanna.

And, forgetting all the shit and misery that had brought things to this point. And that Johanna had, just the night before, dumped me, no matter how nice it had gone down.

I drank some coffee and made a foul mess in the toilet. I was still drunk. I showered, to wash it all away, to little avail. While I was under the cold water, Johanna sent me a text, telling me to meet her at the bank to close our joint account and split the money.

I met Johanna at the bank. She was waiting for me at the customer service desk, a scowl cut in her pale Renaissance face like the slashings of a madman at an art museum. The bank woman was anxious, poised on the edge of her seat. I doubt Johanna had said anything to her, but she needn't have. Her face told the story.

"Hi," I said. Johanna didn't look my way nor did she reply.

"So, we're closing the joint account?" the bank woman said. Her voice quavered.

"Yes," I said.

We provided the necessary account numbers and identification. The woman fiddled nervously with the keyboard, flushed and flustered, and finally, closed the account.

"OK, so now you want to open individual accounts and transfer the money fifty-fifty?"

"Do mine first," Johanna said, "so I can get out here."

"Yes ma'am."

When the woman finished, Johanna snatched her paperwork and new ATM card and rushed from the bank.

The woman seemed to melt with relief. She smiled thinly at me.

"Ok, let's do yours now."

"Ok."

She worked with ease this time. When she was done, she looked at me.

"I know how it is. I've been through the same thing. If there's anything I can do, let me know."

"Thank you."

"I mean," she emphasized, "with your account."

"I knew what you meant."

I went home, but Johanna wasn't there. I lay down on the sofa and wondered what would happen next. After an hour I sent her a text and asked her to come back. She said she wasn't ready yet. I waited. Another hour passed, and she pulled in the driveway. I sat up. She barged through the door and blew past me.

"Please, I want to talk to you."

She lay on the bed, turned on the TV, and folded her arms tight. Then she started screaming.

I had hurt her like no one else had ever done. I had betrayed her. I was a liar and a cheat and I was taking advantage of her. And she pressed me for every detail of my encounter with Melissa. How old was she? What did she look like? Did she let me fuck her in the ass?

What? I refused. I didn't want to tell her any of that. Why did she need to know? It would only upset her more. But she insisted, and I finally relented and told her the how and the where, and how old Melissa was.

"Some little fucking whore! How long have you been hooking up with her?"

"I never met her before in my life!"

"You're full of shit!"

I apologized all that I could. I buried my head in my hands and cried.

"You're faking it," she said. "You don't love me."

"Yes, I do! I fucked up, but I do love you!"

"No you don't. You don't love me. But you'll be sorry when I'm gone. You'll never find anyone as good as me."

And so it went on, all that day, and into the night. I apologized a hundred times. And she hardened her resolve a hundred times more. Finally, I gave up and collapsed on the sofa. It was about eleven at night. I fell asleep quickly, but it didn't last. I couldn't sleep most of the night. I was still a wreck on Sunday.

This went on for two more weeks, whenever our kids were away or asleep—my apologies, her accusations, her grief, her threats to throw me out then and there, and a lot of tears—more shed by me than by her.

And then I suddenly realized I hadn't used a condom with Melissa.

"Oh my god," Johanna said. "You fucked this strange girl and you didn't use a rubber? What, are you out of your mind?"

"I told you, I was really drunk. It didn't even occur to me."

At this point Johanna softened.

"You better go get tested. For everything."

"Shit."

I went to the local AIDS clinic. The guy told me I needed to wait ninety days to get a good test.

"That's how long it takes to get an accurate reading on the virus. Sooner than that, you might get a false negative, and go away never knowing you have it."

Back at home, things changed quickly. Johanna was soon trying out new makeup and a new diet program, neither of which she needed. She was obviously trying to make herself more attractive to me. I found it very sad.

We tiptoed around each other for another week. Then one Saturday she came to me, smiling.

"I don't want you to go," she whispered. "This whole thing made me realize how much I really love you. Let's just try to forget about it and move on."

I felt relief. And a strange unease, because after this month of hell, I thought I should go.

I thought I wanted to.

But I stayed. Things got a little better. I felt the love for her again. The ninety days passed, and my AIDS test came back negative. We could have sex again, and took to it like maniacs. We had some fun, some good times with the kids, some family barbeques out on the back deck.

But I had run out of money, and between my bills and child support there was little I could contribute to the house. It was the pit of the recession and there were no jobs for me, of course. Johanna grew impatient with me. I know she expected me to find something to bring in some money. But there were no jobs to be found with so many people in the same floundering boat. And no sense in giving up my Unemployment for some menial job that paid less. She started throwing it up in my face, the money. I was indignant, as it had only been a few months that I wasn't pulling my weight, but I was doing everything around the house—the yard, the shopping, the laundry, and most of the cooking. But it was more than that. She hadn't gotten past Melissa. She didn't trust me. I began to feel like I was being watched. I joined Facebook, at her urging, and she had questions, too many questions, about the people I friended, especially girls I had known in high school. She made ugly comments about them. It made no sense when she had three times the friends I did, and at least half of them were guys she knew in high school and college. Many of which I'm sure she had fucked. She made a lot of comments, not all of them funny, interjected in my conversations with other people.

Her mood worsened. It was back to the beginning, again, the door slamming, the curt responses—or no responses. I knew the damage was irreparable, and that I had to leave.

I just didn't know how.

Jack proved to be the catalyst, again.

We were having a Facebook ball-busting session. A couple of middle-aged fools cutting down each other's manliness with wit and innuendo. We were having a lot fun with it. Then Jack countered one of my claims with the retort, "Yeah, your girlfriends down at the bar will really go for that".

About a second later Johanna chimed in. She'd been following the conversation in silence.

"Oh, that's great. That's just what I wanted to hear," she wrote.

Fuck, I thought. I hurried into the bedroom.

"He's just joking, okay? We're just busting chops and playing around."

"I don't believe you, and I don't trust you," Johanna hissed. Her kids were in the living room watching TV. "And I don't like that guy Jack. I don't want you talking to him anymore!"

"What? What the hell are you talking about?"

"Yes you do."

"No, I don't."

"You're seeing somebody else!"

"Oh my god, I am not. That thing with the girl was a one-time drunken thing. I thought we moved on from that. Why the hell don't you trust me? I haven't been out uptown at all since then, except with you. So you know I'm not out trying to pick up girls or anything."

"That doesn't matter. I know you're up to something."

"How? What makes you think so?"

"I know a secret."

"What? What secret?"

"I saw that email you wrote him back in June. Where you ripped me to shreds." She began to cry. "I've never had anyone say anything about me like those things you said to him about me. You don't know how much that hurt me."

"Oh my god. I was drunk and pissed off and venting with a trusted friend. I wouldn't have ever said anything like that to you. Nor have I ever."

"And then you talked about finding some other girl. Well good luck, buster, because you'll never find anyone as good as me."

"That was stupid guy-bragging. Holy shit. And anyway, how did you wind up reading it?"

"I came out to check on you and you were passed out on the sofa. I didn't mean to read anything; I just saw it as I passed."

Things began to fall in place.

"No, you didn't. You looked at it on purpose. That laptop was facing the wall, practically in the corner. You couldn't just pass it and accidentally see anything. And how long ago was this? Almost six months? Why didn't you say anything?"

Johanna looked away.

"Well I know why. Because you knew you were wrong to spy on me. And to judge me based on it ever since."

I threw on my coat and took a long walk. It was November, and I was shaking; not from the cold, but from rage. I went through a half dozen cigarettes before I calmed down.

I knew I had to leave.

Johanna obliged me a few days later. She told me I had to go. I didn't know where, since landlords typically didn't rent apartments to unemployed people. She gave me six weeks to figure it out. But a few days later she flipped out and demanded I get out as soon as possible. I got lucky; I knew a girl who managed some small apartment buildings. She trusted me for the rent money, and rented me the place I'm in now. My kids cried when they found out. Johanna never said goodbye to them. It was horrible, and I felt guilty, and I still do. My marriage failed, things failed with Johanna, and my kids got hurt twice.

And Johanna told her family and everyone we knew together that I cheated on her and took advantage of her, and there's not much I can say, because that's all you see when you look at the surface of it.

Maybe things would have worked out if I hadn't fucked Melissa. Or maybe I would have been trapped with Johanna, unable to leave. Johanna still loved me when I left. And I still loved her, although, despite everything, I was glad to go.

I wish I could turn back the clock, back to the good times we had before the nightmare struck.

*   *   *

The second tequila is done, and I see that I've poured a third. I have to slow down or I'll be passed out by nine. I make some coffee, and while it's cooling, I step outside for a cigarette. It's still half-light. The days are slowly getting longer. But it's still cold. The few remaining plow-drifts of snow have shrunk and blackened. I examine the edge of the woods beyond the cul-de-sac. The brittle, frosted carpet of dead leaves is undisturbed. No one is sleeping in the trees.

Heading back inside I meet the pretty blonde girl from next-door heading out. She's stunning—dressed up, made up, hair done in long flowing curls. Despite the cold, she doesn't have a coat or even a jacket. Instead she's wrapped in a long silky blue dress that matches her eyes; high-heeled sandals, and a black shoulder wrap to cover her bare arms. In one hand she clutches a tiny black purse and in the other, a bottle of wine. I can't help it—I stop before her, and stare.

"Big date tonight?" I stammer.

"Something like that," she says, with a grin that's silly, seductive, and vulnerable all at once.

"Well, any guy that doesn't fall in love with you from just looking at you isn't a man." I'm a cocky bastard when I drink tequila.

She smiles at that but says nothing, and I feel the falling away of pretense and obstacles, and a sense of possibility. But that passes on the wind, and when it's gone I realize what I said to her was my heart speaking. I don't know if she caught it, but I'm embarrassed. I say goodbye and she eases into her little car and drives off while I hurry back inside. And there I feel the awful loss of magic. But I'm grateful for the glimpse of it she gave me.

*　　*　　*

Another drink and an hour later and that forlorn feeling has given way to bitterness and lust. Thinking about Melissa, and seeing that beautiful girl—I'm fucking horny. And I'm fucking pissed. I'm going uptown for some pussy tonight.

I have to prepare. First I struggle for nearly an hour to clear out my bowels. Another bloody mess. More wasted time. And once more, a finger jamming the swollen flesh back inside. I'm sick of it.

I shower, I shave, I lay out some clothes. My best jeans, some cool black shoes, a white tee shirt and a thin black sweater over it. I regard myself in the bathroom mirror. A little gel in the hair; fingers through it, affecting a stylish, jagged mess. I look pretty good. A little pale, though. It's all the blood I've lost, of course.

I throw on my three-quarter length black leather jacket. Sleek, weathered, and supple. It's my favorite jacket. And it has deep pockets, for my wallet, phone, keys, cigarettes, condoms-- and the revolver, because possibilities aren't forthcoming for me in young, pretty blue eyes any more. They're to be found in cold blue steel, instead.

I don't call or text anyone. Not Gene or the dudes in the building or any of the other guys I go drinking with from time to time. Right now, I just want to go. I tear through the doorway, fumble with the lock, and hurry across the near-empty parking lot. I light a cigarette on the run. A blue wake of smoke trails behind me, slowly rising, and then vanishing, as ephemeral as the years past and the memories that drive me uptown, in search of some kind of succor.

The weight of the gun causes my jacket to swing out and in with the rhythm of my pace, slapping my thigh. I have to bury my hand in the pocket to hold it steady.

I stop at the first place I reach, a small pub. A light crowd mingles in the midst of the half dark of the open floor and the tables lining the walls. The bartenders draw beers and mix drinks under the glare of narrow beams of light. There is a steady murmur of conversation. Bits of old songs drone from the speaker system while the flatscreens on the walls sparkle with sports highlights and streaming commentary. A girl laughs loud and high. Someone hoots. Things are just warming up.

"Tequila and coke, with lime," I tell the bartender. I know this guy. He knows the drink. He has his hand on the tequila before I open my mouth. But how does he know that it's tequila tonight, and not my usual vodka? Is it written on my face? I pay him the seven dollars. Succor doesn't come cheap in this town. But I'm not, either. I give him a two dollar tip. He nods. He doesn't say much, if anything, ever. I don't care.

I sip my drink, and suddenly feel like I want someone around. I text a message that I'm uptown in this pub, looking for company, and I send it to Gene, the Dudes, another guy, and a girl I dated once right after I got divorced that I'm somewhat friends with. I don't expect anyone to show; they've probably all made plans, or are ensconced on their sofas with their loved ones in front of the television for the night. Except for the Dudes, I think; the Dudes might show.

I hope someone shows. I didn't care before, but now I do. I want someone to stand with, to be with, so people don't know the truth: I'm alone. So when the strangers look at my face from across the room they see a guy laughing and talking, and not the grim, haunted look I've seen looking back at me from too many barroom mirrors.

I'm done with my drink. Was that my fourth already tonight? It doesn't feel like it. All the caffeine and sugar in the Coke keeps my head clear—I don't feel like I've had anything to drink at all. The bartender glances my way and I nod and he brings me another. Seven dollars and another two dollar tip. Good service, but I wish the lithe blond honey of a barmaid would come down to my end of the bar and serve me. Of course, from faraway, I can see her tight ass. Up close, it would just be waist-up. But she's not just another hot body. She makes a damn good Bloody Mary, too. And any other kind of drink I've ever asked her to make for me. You know what I mean? I chuckle. I'm carrying on a conversation with myself in my head.

I think I am, anyway. I look to my left and my right. An old fart guy and an empty stool, respectively. The old fart guy is beefy, half-bald, and has a sad face. He's sipping something dark in a pint glass. Not so dark as a Guinness; maybe a Sam Adams. I hate beer. It gives you indigestion and makes you fat. I should tell him that, the old fart. I look closer and realize the guy is probably five or ten years younger than me. He just looks older because he's dressed like a lawyer. Maybe he is a lawyer. Maybe I should ask him about the statutes regarding illegal firearms. Concealed, no less. He looks up from his pint like he wants to talk. I look away, feigning interest in the football highlights on the flatscreen. I don't want to talk to him. This is a bad spot I'm standing in. I need to sidle up to some women. But there aren't any at the bar. Just a few at the tables and some more in mixed groups out on the floor. That's okay; it's still early and I'm just warming up.

My phone vibrates. It's a text from Gene. He's beat from class and a paper and isn't coming out. I didn't think he would. I wonder if he's still mad at me. If he is, so be it; I'm at peace with it. Those exact words sound in my head: "I'm at peace with it."

I must be drunk. In my head, at least. My body feels fine, though. Funny what Coke in a drink can do.

This place sucks. Time to move on. I nod to my silent bartender and drop another dollar on the bar. So when they ask, what kind of a guy was he? he'll say, he was a good tipper.

I have to have something, you know? Something good that people say about me. Even if they don't know who I am.

I hit the street, where the lights, the energy of the sinewy, hurrying crowd and the cold air hit me like a shot of adrenaline. The buzz is on, and I'm part of it. I grin, latch on to the wave, and sail on down the Strip.

I marvel at all the pussy. The legs, the heels, the short jackets, the no-jackets; the clinging jeans, skimpy dresses, the undulating hips. The sweaty ass cheeks bisected by the thin lines of thongs that I can't see but know are there. I'm going mad. And the cleavage, pushed up and over low-cut tops, dresses, blouses, sweaters. Swelling tits cradled in Victoria's Secret wire and lace. Pretty young faces; some innocent, some whorish, with mascara and glossed pouty lips and bouncy, shining hair, pulled up, on the shoulder, or down the back. I'm going mad. I've gone mad. A trembling ache grows in the pit of my loins, rippling outward through my torso and along my limbs. A pain older than time; a laughing, mocking rat gnawing at all men's guts, urging us forward, at any and all cost—insanity, murder, heartbreak, death—to fuck. Maybe it would be better to cut off your own nuts and find a little peace. But no; a man could emasculate himself but if he didn't castrate his mind he'd go insane at the first piece of ass passing on the street. Because the urge is imprinted in the brain, and without the balls, the frustration would be exponential. A man would have no recourse but suicide.

But these thoughts have no place here in the midst of this mini-Sodom. This is no place for philosophy. I wonder what expression these ruminations have etched across my face. Not a good one, I'm sure. I stop for a cigarette. I force a half-smile, because no one wants to fuck a madman.

The good feeling gradually returns. Along with confidence. I'm going to fuck me one of these hot little bitches tonight, I know it. But first I need another drink.

I start to move, and then I freeze. Is that Johanna across the street?

There's a woman and a guy hand in hand and she has Johanna's body, Johanna's coat and Johanna's hair, but with red highlights. She has it pulled back and up and that one lock hangs down over her temple and cheek like it always did.

Shit, is that her?

My heart clatters in a painful tempo against the underside of my ribs. I have to clutch a bench to keep from falling. Some prick laughs at me as he passes, some remark about not handling my liquor, and I hiss a curse at his receding back. I turn and strain to see this maybe-Johanna, this laughing woman with another guy, but she's fading from sight, she's turning the corner, she's gone.

And that's where she should stay, gone, but she isn't. She wrote me back tonight but I didn't reply. I should say something to her. But I don't know what.

No, I shouldn't. Let her go and forget her.

I can't. I've been emasculated but not castrated.

What do I do now?

But I don't have to decide. The Dudes arrive and decide for me.

"Hey man, what's up? I got your text."

"Man, I'm glad to see you guys."

"Wanna hit the Lizard?"

"That's fine. Let's go."

We hurry down toward the end of the Strip to the Leapin' Lizard. I feel so much better, not to be alone. The Dudes are good guys. And they're a lot of fun. Ryan is the loud one, drinks heavily, and when he's drunk, relentlessly hits on girls. Mark is quiet, mellow, and has a girlfriend, Erica. He brought her out tonight. She's a nice girl. She's good to him, and sweet. I like them all.

The din is incredible at the Lizard. A band is warming up, doing sound checks, cutting into the piped soundtrack which is barely audible over the rush of shouts and laughter. The four-sided bar is packed and the bartenders are scuttling back and forth, drawing beers and tipping handfuls of fifth bottles into ice-filled glasses. A clutch of waitresses are shuttling trays of appetizers to people perched at the high cocktail tables. Some drunk women in business suits, leftovers from the Happy Hour crowd, are out on the dance floor, hopping about to some 80s song. I give them a quick look-over—nothing there for me. They look bad. I can see they have husbands, kids, more hemorrhoids than me, and their misery will be compounded tomorrow when they wake up with the kind of wicked hangover they haven't had in a decade.

But I like the Lizard. It has something for everybody: a restaurant, a bar with a bandstand and dance floor, a sports bar off to the side, and a cigar bar off to another side, for the sophisticated crowd.

And is Johanna here, somewhere?

"What are you guys drinking? I got first round," I cry.

Ryan and Mark want some beers. Erica just wants a Coke. I don't think I've ever seen her have a drink.

I slip through the bar crowd with the skill of a master carpenter working a chisel into soft wood. I hail a bartender on the basis of recognition. Two beers, a Coke, and a tequila and tonic. I tip him well. I pass the Coke and the beers to my companions and scan the bar. The rat is gnawing again. I need to get laid.

I feel like I'll die if I don't.

"Let's find us some women, dude," I say to Ryan. His eyes are rolling in his head. He must have had most of that case of beer they brought in earlier.

"Hell yeah!" he shouts.

He won't be much help.

We work on our drinks and talk. I can't make much sense of what anyone is saying, but it's not because I'm hopelessly drunk. When it's this loud, I can't hear individual sounds. It all gets lost in the roar. This doesn't help me with women, either. I can only nod and smile and hope it's at the right time.

Although in a place like this, conversation isn't that important

Ryan makes a sudden beeline for a pair of young girls nearby, and I follow. Mark and Erica exchange knowing looks, then begin kissing, turning inward on themselves like a snake eating its own tail.

The two girls are blond, pretty, and look a bit different, possibly foreign. They're dressed casually in jeans and sweaters and jackets, but they're still hot. Ryan picks one and begins shouting in her ear. Whatever he says, she likes it, and starts laughing. Soon they're face to face, talking intently. I look at the other girl, smile, and shrug. A blur of thoughts are racing through my mind, but I can't find anything to say to her. I feel self-conscious, because she's so young—and I'm so old. I try to look her over without looking like I am. Her hair is very long, and straight. She looks Latin, even though she's blond. She has a black cap on, squared down tight on her head, the bill slung low over her eyes. She looks like she's hiding behind it. But she's not afraid to speak first.

"You're not like your friend, you're more quiet."

At least I think that's what she says. I have to watch her lips carefully to make sure.

"Well, not really, once I get started I can't shut up. Where are you from?"

I can't make out her words this time.

"What?" I cry. She leans forward and shouts in my ear.

"I'm from Brazil, and my friend is from Argentina."

"Oh, so you speak Portuguese and she speaks Spanish. How do you understand each other?"

See how smart I am, I know the language difference. I'm afraid to be blunt, so I pretend to try making an intellectual connection.

When she leans forward this time, her lips touch my ear. An accident? My body doesn't care. My flesh springs alive like a fast-motion movie shot of a flowering meadow.

"We both speak English."

Of course they do. It was a stupid question.

"Are you a student?"

"No, I am an au pair. We are both au pairs."

I run with this. I talk about how there are so many au pairs around, because this is such an affluent area. The bars are crawling with them. I dated one once, a girl from Switzerland. We were born on the same day. This was a long time ago, but I don't tell her how long.

"Where are you from in Brazil?"

She names a city, but I can't hear her. But I know she didn't say Sao Paolo. I tell her I'd love to go to Brazil, especially Sao Paolo. It's stuck in my mind because I've seen all this Brazilian porno on the internet, shot in Sao Paolo.

"Sao Paolo isn't a nice place."

Ryan saves me by suggesting a round of shots. I ask for more tequila. My friend asks for vodka. Ryan bludgeons past us and up to the bar.

Fuck it, I can't think of anything witty or right to say. Or anything at all. So I try to get her to talk instead.

"What's your name," I ask.

"Maria, what's yours?"

I tell her. "So how many kids are you taking care of? Do you enjoy it?"

She shouts in my ear for a while, brushing against my cheek with her lips, her hair, and her hat. I don't hear most of what she says, and I don't care. She's driving me mad. I want her badly. How? Dancing. If I can get her to dance, I can do it.

Ryan returns with the shots. We toast, and suck them down.

"You don't take salt and lime with yours," she shouts.

"That's for kids," I say. She laughs at that.

I quickly snatch that hat from her head. A hidden layer of blond hair cascades in a plunging cataract over her shoulders. And the whole of her face is brought into the light.

Now I know why she wore the hat. She's stunning. If she didn't hide it, she would have no peace from men.

"Give me my hat," she says, although I don't hear it. She's embarrassed. I hand it back, and she stuffs it full of hair and pulls it low over her eyes.

"You're beautiful," I say. She looks away, smiling.

I lean in close to her face.

"Let's dance," I say.

She looks me over intently.

"How old are you?"

"How old do you think I am?"

"Thirty?"

In a rush of ego and hubris I laugh and announce, "I'm forty-seven!"

Her face darkens.

"My father is forty-eight."

I scramble to save the situation.

"Well, at least I'm younger than him!"

But it's too late. She tugs at her friend's arm and talks into her ear. The other girl looks at me, surprised. Maria turns away and fades into the crowd. Her friend says something to Ryan and breaks away from him to follow her, and they're gone.

Ryan is too drunk to understand what happened.

"Where'd they go?" he shouts.

"Ladies room."

"They coming back?"

"I don't think so."

He grins, and shrugs. He's too drunk to care. But I'm not. He wanders off, in search of more prey, but I don't follow this time. I move up against the bar and order a drink. I'm starting to fade, so I order another tequila and Coke.

"Fuck it," I say, but no one hears me.

*　　*　　*

It's later, and everything is droning on. The people, the music. There is a drink in my hand. I'm leaning up against the bar, bracing myself with my elbows. One of my feet is on the rail. Time has passed, but I'm not sure how much. I remember going outside for a cigarette, and staring at a girl until she said, "What the fuck?" and turned and stormed away. A minute later a blond girl bummed a smoke from me. I looked closely to see if she was Melissa. She wasn't.

Melissa. Maybe she's in town tonight. Maybe I can find her. I should go back outside the club where I met her. Maybe she's there. This time I could take her home and not have to fuck her in her car.

A girl presses up against me, trying to get to the bar. I slide to the left and give her some space. I look at her, and she smiles broadly. She's not a girl; she's a woman in her forties. Short blond hair. Not pretty, but not bad. She starts talking to me like she knows me. Did I talk to her earlier? Or on some other night?

"I'm Kathy," she says. I'm able to make that out above the din.

"Hi Kat," I say. Behind her are a few more women, younger, in their thirties. One looks really nice. She's looking at me strangely. I don't recognize her. I can't decide what her look means.

Kathy orders a drink, but doesn't go away. She starts rattling off words in my ear. They don't make any sense. I reply, not knowing what I'm saying. This goes on for a while, and slowly, my head clears a bit.

Kathy is hanging on me, but for some reason, I don't like her.

"Why is your friend staring at me like that?" I ask.

Kathy yells something I don't understand.

I pick up this, however: "You're standing here looking mad," she says. But she's smiling when she says it. If I do look mad, it's not putting her off.

"It's my bar face," I shout. "And this is my regular face," I continue, and cross my eyes and stick out my tongue. Kathy chokes on her drink, laughing. I glance back. Her friend is still looking at me in that same, strange way. I still can't figure it out. Maybe she didn't like my bar face.

But Kathy does and she's coming on to me but I don't like her. She has a nice body. She has nice clothes.

It's her hair. It's too short. Cut the way a middle-aged woman will cut it when she just can't be bothered with it anymore. When she stops being a girl. When she's old.

"Excuse me, I gotta go have a smoke," I say. She says something, and lays a napkin over my glass so the bartenders won't take it.

My head clears a little more in the crisp, freezing air. I light a cigarette with shaking hands. I check my phone. No messages. I check the time. Another hour until closing time. The street is teeming with people, desperate for their last chance of the night. As I am. Where are you, Melissa?

Where are you, Johanna?

About half a dozen women, laughing like crazy, and a guy, roaring drunk, prance up to the door. I know them; we hung out drinking a few weeks ago. They're about five years younger than me and went to my high school. I tried to make a date with one of them, Eileen, but she wasn't interested. I caught her friend, Debra, who's married, kissing Brad, the guy. He's divorced and out here from L.A. for a few weeks visiting his kids. And making out with old girlfriends from high school.

When they see me coming, Debra and Brad look at me anxiously and try to wave me away.

"What's up guys?" I say.

Debra grabs me by the collar of my jacket and pulls me aside.

"Don't say anything, we're just old friends from high school, it was just a friendly kiss, I'm a married woman, you know?"

"I don't give a shit, Deb. I really don't."

Debra is hot in tight jeans and high heels, like last time. But Eileen looks classy in a long black dress. She sees me and looks away. I follow them inside, around to the other side of the bar from Kathy. I catch a glimpse of Kathy watching me but pretend not to see her.

I insinuate myself in the midst of them. I like Eileen. And I'd like to fuck Debra. When Brad's drunken fog parts for a moment, he recognizes me, and, laughing, tries to push me away. He says something but I can't make it out.

"Ease up, man," I say, "I saw nothing, I know nothing, and I'm not going to say anything."

He backs off. I get another tequila and tap his beer bottle with my glass. He looks at me like he doesn't know me anymore, but he smiles anyway.

I hang out with them for a while. The band has worked itself into a frenzy, slamming out one 80s dance tune after another. I can't hear anything else anymore. I work my way slowly to Eileen's side. She's leaning against the bar shelf that lines the wall. She doesn't say anything. She didn't say much last time, either. The low-cut dress bares her shoulders and much of her chest. She has small breasts. Her breasts and chest are covered with freckles.

"You have a lot of freckles," I say. "They're cute."

I lean forward and lick her chest.

"Taste good, too," I laugh.

She smiles a little. Her eyes roll. She's very drunk.

"So what's new?" I ask. She shrugs. "What are you drinking," I say, despite the bottle of beer clearly visible in her hand.

"No more drinks for me tonight," she says. "I'm calling a cab and going home." She lurches forward, then staggers back. I throw out my arm to catch her. She falls against my palm then rockets forward, past her friends, into the crowd, and toward the bathrooms in the back.

Debra comes up to me.

"What's with Eileen?

"She's calling a cab and going home."

Debra rejoins the other girls and when the band strikes the first chords of a Bon Jovi song, they scream and surge onto the dance floor. Debra tries to drag Brad along, but he can barely stand. Instead he leans on the main bar, watching them, grinning slack-jawed and stupidly, like a cow.

"Fugg this," I say to myself, and move out on to the floor with the girls. Am I suddenly completely drunk, too? Yes. It hits me like a sack of wet sand. I don't care. Because I can dance pretty good. Check this out, bitches.

I dance right into the midst of them and show what I can do. I can dance well. That's right. Spin, spin, grind, grind. One girl grabs my ass, I don't know which one. They're flashing past too quickly. Where is Debra? I want to fuck that hot-assed cheating bitch.

There she is, at the bar, making out with Brad again. Fucking whore. Where's your husband? Home watching your kids, that's where. Wouldn't he like to know what you do on Girls Night Out.

Eileen passes, working her arms into her jacket, fumbling in her purse for a cigarette. She moves like Johanna. Fuck Johanna. Fuck Eileen. Fuck Debra, and Kathy, and Maria from Brazil. Eileen crashes through the door bent on catching her cab. I should follow, have a smoke with her. Maybe she'll take me back to her place in the cab. At least she's divorced and not some married, cheating bitch. It's almost closing. I gotta hook up quick, otherwise it's a long cold walk home alone. Yes sir.

The girls are moving. Where are they going? Off the floor, leaving me alone. Well me too, I don't want to stand here all by myself like a jackass. They're pulling on their jackets, checking their purses, talking, talking to me, but I can't hear what they're saying.

"Are you going home?" They answer but I still can't hear them. They're helping Brad into his long coat. He can't hold his eyes open. His legs are buckling. Two of the girls are holding him up.

All of them are leaving. But Debra is still leaning against the bar, sucking on a beer. She's not putting on a coat. Just me and her now?

A blond girl from the group comes up and waves her finger under my nose.

"You better watch yourself, I know your face! You better not let anything happen to her!"

"What the fuck are you talking about?" She goes on, but I can't hear her words, but I understand. Debra is staying and this bitch doesn't want me to fuck her. Or, if I do fuck her, I should not murder her.

What a nasty bitch.

"You want my address and phone to track me down if anything happens to her?"

"I don't need that. I know your face! You just make sure she gets in a cab home."

"On my honor, I promise."

Fucking crazy bitch. Finally, she gets out of my face, and the entire group leaves. I turn to Debra.

I can't stand too well. I lean against the bar beside her.

"Want a beer?"

"Sure."

I get her a beer. She pulls on it while I sip what remains of my drink. What am I drinking? I can't even tell. All I taste is alcohol. It may be vodka and club. Without the club.

The band strikes up another 80s crowd pleaser. Billy Idol, maybe? It's mostly just a roar. Debra grabs my hand.

"Let's dance."

We're out on the floor. The crowd has thinned, there's enough room to move around now. She's a good dancer. I grab her hips and twist them, I spin her, but when I move in to grind, she pulls away. I follow, catch up with her, we dance some more, spin, try to grind, she pulls away. This goes on a few more times. OK, she'll dance, but she won't touch me. I give up and just dance. Then I'm turning, turning, and each time, I see two young guys at the bar, near where we were drinking, eyeing us with mild hostility.

What the fuck is this bullshit?

"Hey, those two guys at the bar, they're giving us dirty looks. Are they like your husband's friends or something?"

Debra looks over my shoulder at them.

"I don't know them."

I don't believe her.

Then a young blond girl joins us, making it a threesome. She's moving so fast, and I'm so drunk, I can barely make out her face, but she looks hot and pretty. And she's wild; throwing herself at both of us. Maybe she wants a real threesome? Drunk as I am, I feel a stirring in my pants at the idea.

Debra steps back.

"Dance with her," she says, and moves away.

Fine, go fuck yourself. This girl is hot.

The girl is wild. I grab her and grind my crotch against hers. She's wearing a thin skirt and I can feel everything. I'm hard and pushing it against her like I'm fucking her. We're spinning around and around and she's pulling at me, throwing her head back, tossing her long hair in circles.

Holy shit I'm going to fuck this chick tonight.

The madness has me. I spin her around, wrap one arm around the front of her waist and plant my other palm between her shoulder blades and push, forcing her into a standing doggy-style position. Then I start slamming my crotch against her ass, fucking her to the beat of the song. She slams back against me in kind. Yeah, yeah! The bass player is right in front of us and he's watching this, eyes bulging and mouth agape. As is everyone else left at the bar, I imagine.

It's crazy. I'm going crazy. I grab both her shoulders and pull her in harder. Then I grab both her hips. My bones are cracking. My crotch is bulging, it's sore. My cock is hard and it's pounding her between her ass cheeks, just beneath the thin fabric of her skirt and whatever's beneath it. I start fondling her bare legs, working my way up. My hands are on her ass cheeks. I must be exposing her ass to the crowd but I can't see down there. She's wearing a thong. She spins around when I run my fingers over her wet pussy lips.

She says something but I can't hear it, of course. We're right in front of one of the speakers. I pull her face to mine. She's very young. Maybe twenty-five.

"Let's get out of here," I say.

"I can't. My fiancée is over there in the sports bar."

My loins are churning with a mix of desire, anguish, anger, and a sense of imminent danger.

"OK, bye!" I cry and move away from her as quick as I can. I fumble my way to the bar, looking for my drink. I can't find it. I pick up a half-full glass abandoned on the side bar and empty it. Whiskey and soda. I gag.

The lights come up and the band shuts down. Closing time. The bass player sets down his instrument and comes over to me.

"Man, that just made my night, watching you and that chick. But where the fuck is she? You gotta fuck that chick, she's fucken primed and ready."

"That little fucking whore is over there in the sports bar with her fiancée. All I did was get her all hot and wet for him."

"What a fucking slut. Well, rock on, dude. Maybe tomorrow night, huh?"

"Yeah, maybe."

It's fucked up, it's all fucked up. Everything is fucked up. I'm so goddamned frustrated. But I'm not really mad at the girl. I feel like she couldn't give me everything, but at least she gave me something.

Yeah, blue balls.

I see Debra going out the door with the two guys that were watching us.

Everything is all fucked up. I need a cigarette. I follow them.

The air is cold and wet like a sopping rag left outside overnight. I'm shaking and I have to button up my jacket. Debra and the guys are already half a block down the street. I want to give chase, but there is a tap on my shoulder. I turn. It's Kathy, and the girl that stares. Kathy is smiling and the other girl is still looking at me strangely, like I'm some kind of animal she can't identify.

Shit, they saw the whole dance, didn't they?

"I put a napkin on your last drink," Kathy says, "but they took it away anyway."

"OK, thanks for that. It's allright, I hadda 'nuff ta drink."

"Well, we have to go now."

They're waiting. What does she want from me? What does the other one want?

"OK, good talkin to ya. Drive safe!" I say, and turn to light a smoke and watch Debra and her friends retreat from the scene. Kathy and the other girl head off in the other direction; I can hear their heels clattering on the pavement behind me. They gradually fade away.

Debra and the guys are two blocks away now. They pause at a corner. Then she takes both their hands, and they turn right, disappear down the intersecting block, and are gone.

I want to scream after her, but I'm surrounded by all the people slowly pouring from the bar, lighting cigarettes, staggering, huddling for warmth, laughing uproariously. A young couple embraces and kisses, and it hurts to watch them. I turn away.

It's a lucky move because I'm just in time to face a big, angry young guy rushing straight at me.

"What were you doing with my girlfriend, you old motherfucker?"

It's the Fiancée.

He shoves me brutally with both hands and I'm thrown back against a parking meter, which saves me from hitting the deck. But it hurts like a knife between the shoulder blades. I bounce forward, and he hollers before rushing in again.

"You were feeling up my woman, bitch!"

This time I shove back.

"Get the fuck off me!"

We grapple for a few seconds, and then we're torn apart. Two bouncers have us both in headlocks. I'm not fighting it, but

Fiancée is; he's kicking out, and he's drunk; he kicks with both legs at once and almost falls to the ground.

"Cool it!" shouts the bouncer that has him, bouncing him up and down.

"Get the fuck outta here," my bouncer says, and lets me go. I hurry away, passing Fiancée, who cuts me a murderous look. I reach the first corner and turn right. I gotta get the fuck away from this guy. I can do it, I'm sure; I know the town well. I cross the street and slip into a narrow alley that climbs a rise and opens to the next block. I make it, and no sign of him. I pause. My heart is racing, my lungs are fighting for air, and my head is spinning with adrenaline and alcohol. What fucking bullshit. Little fucking bitch, got me in this shit.

And that whore, Debra. I'm not good enough to fuck? I'm not good enough?

"I'm not good enough?!" I scream. But no one hears me. I'm all alone on the street.

In a fury, I storm to the end of the block, turn left, race down another block, and make a right. Then I'm on my street, five blocks from home.

And here I almost collapse. Too much to drink, man. My legs nearly give out. And my hemorrhoid pops out of my ass, chafing against the inner seam of my jeans.

"Shit," I mutter.

This happens when I get extremely drunk. My whole body goes slack, and my rectum relaxes, and it can't hold my piles in anymore. There's nothing I can do until I get home and lube it up with ointment and push it back in. I can't drop my pants in the street and stick my finger up my ass. It won't work, anyway, without the lube. I begin to walk, slowly, gingerly, so I don't rub it too much and start it to bleed.

Then a car races up and screeches to a halt beside me. The door flies open and Fiancée leaps out.

"You're dead, motherfucker!" he screams.

Then I remember that I have a gun in my pocket.

But he's on me too fast, and this time, with fists swinging. I throw mine up to block his and dodge and duck and nearly scream from the pain of my piles tearing inside the seat of my pants. There's a dull impact on the side of my head, another in my side, and then I start swinging too. We're gasping and locking arms and then I smack him in the mouth. His lip splits and blood pours from it. Then I feel another shot to the head; it doesn't hurt, but I feel my whole body blow out like a fuse. I drop.

When the lights come up, I'm on my back on the wet sidewalk and he's kicking me in the legs and the ribs. I don't feel anything. But now everything is much clearer.

"Yeah, yeah, that's it, you old bitch, that's it!"

I shove my right hand in my pocket and wrap it around the gun. It's ice cold and hard and it has four bullets in it.

But I don't pull it out.

Why not?

Isn't this what I got it for, because the whole world is beating the shit out of me?

"You should go now," I say, cold and flat. I stare at the guy through bleeding eyes.

He doesn't understand. But he stops anyway. I don't think it's because I have one hand stuffed menacingly in my pocket, though. I think it's because he suddenly realizes he's drunk and kicking another drunk down on his back on the sidewalk, and maybe he ought to go before the cops come. He looks up and down the street anxiously.

He throws me a glance and hisses, "Motherfucker!" and then hurries to his car.

I'm still gripping the gun.

The door slams, the tires squeal, the car tears down the street, whips around the first corner, and vanishes in a long, fading howl.

I let the gun go. I pull myself to my feet, limb by limb. I'm stiff, but there's no pain. Not even in my ass. But I can feel a thread of blood creeping between my ass cheeks and crawling down my right leg.

I'm standing, but my soul is six feet underground. I am beaten. I am done. I am unwanted. I am alone.

Not even this gun can save me now.

I limp homeward, hands buried in my pockets, and I try not to touch the gun.

It begins to snow.

*　　*　　*

All is a blur: the snow without, and I, within.

I drag myself through the whipping wind and thick wet flakes of the sudden storm. It's a mere three blocks, but it feels like miles. My legs move on their own, bearing the rest of my drunken, limp body. I pass darkened homes, and dimly lit homes, and I wonder if anyone is watching. I wonder what they would think to find me tomorrow on their lawn, facedown and frozen and buried under the snow. A hump in the yard they might ignore, peering through a frosted windowpane, while they sip their morning coffee. Something the neighbor's dog would sniff at until shooed away. Something that might lie there unnoticed until the sun returned and the snow melts, days hence.

But it won't happen because the legs know the way home, and they rise to the task they've risen to many times before, and they bear me to my door. There, my hands take over, fumbling for the keys, clattering, rattling, cursing and laughing; but the hands know, too, and I'm inside, and once the door is shut and latched then both legs and hands give way, their job is done, and I'm on the floor.

Now the heart must have its moment. With much pounding it raises the body and drags it to the table and forces the mind and the fingers to recall passwords and keyboard layouts and despite much fumbling and groping it opens an email and it types something in reply; something heartfelt and desperate and regrettable. Then it directs the fingers to send this missive and shut the works down before the mind realizes what the heart has done and tries to undo it.

And now, home safe and yearning heart satisfied, it's anyone's game. The mind has shut down, the limbs tremble, the eyes don't see. In this vacuum the stomach cries out for satisfaction. Chips, salsa, chocolate, canned macaroni, pretzels, god-knows-what is shoveled into the mouth, drooling from the sudden onslaught of sensation. It's a long time and a lot of food before the stomach is sated. It always has the last word on nights like this, and I wonder, is it some final impulse of self-preservation, to gorge like this, to fill the stomach with food to slow the absorption of all the booze so it doesn't kill me? Because for some reason, not matter how much I drink, I almost never throw it up.

Then I'm tearing off my clothes. Tearing them off and falling onto the bed and feeling nothing and the room light is still on but the one in my head shuts off, but just before it does, the full weight of knowing that I replied to Johanna hits me and I pass into oblivion sick with regret at what I may have said.

VI.

I don't dream. There is only darkness. When waking comes, it is slow, drawn-out, and much like a dream. I slip between the dark and dream-state for a while.

In the dream-state, I feel the pain. Not from the drinking I've done; that will come later. Just memories and heartbreak, now. What I always feel on weekend mornings, only worse.

On weekend mornings, I used to wake up, and Johanna was there. Asleep on her side in one of my long tee-shirts, her ribs rising and falling in a slow, tidal rhythm. Her back was to me, and I would slowly inch forward and bury my face in the lush fan of her hair. It was downy and carried the scent of fruit. I would breathe it in for a while; her hair, the skin of her neck, her. She would stir slightly at that.

I would awaken to her scent, and the warmth pouring from her. My own breath would come, then, in long, deep draughts, and I would crawl up against her, gently pressing against her back. I would feather my fingertips along her smooth thighs, and a tiny gasp would come from her lips. She would begin to stir; to unfold from sleep, to come alive at my touch. My hands would crawl under the tee-shirt, along her hot skin, pressing gently, tracing a curved path from hip to breast. She would arch her back and press her ass against my hips, urging them forward, and when I slid myself between her warm cheeks, the passion took us.

My grip on her tightened, my hands moved farther and faster, and our breath came fast. We entangled ourselves;

locking, unlocking our limbs, and we made our love. Fast, or slow; mad, or tender. However our hearts spake that morning. With laughter, howls, and often, with tender, whispered words. But it was always good.

After, we lay in our own grease, our tousled hair, the funk and effluvience of our love.

Saying silly things. And eternal declarations.

And in the weekend afternoons, we'd do it again.

This was the Golden Time, before we lived together.

Then she went back to her place, and we were with our kids, but the love played on through the week. Like a record stuck in the same sweet groove of a song. We were never really apart, not for an hour, during the week. The text, the phone, kept us together. It was mostly laughs during the week. And comfort, when things in Life went wrong. And of course teasing, promises, and yearning for the next weekend.

But now, those weekends are gone. Eternity will come, but our declarations are long turned to dust. There is only this: a broken mattress and a cold shadow where she used to lay. Shadowy stains telling of a broken love. And I, with something broke inside, and no hope to mend it.

A hole, where I lost something priceless in the time it took to take a breath.

To know how much I lost is what hurts the most.

*   *   *

It takes time, but I gradually realize I'm not alone in the bed.

But it's not a living thing beside me. Not anymore.

It's cold and hard and wedged up against my swollen asshole.

I've shit the goddamn bed.

It's a measure of how close I've come to dying from drinking too much. First, the piles gave way and then, the colon. After that would come the kidneys, the gall bladder, the liver, the heart. The gradual shutting down of the system. I stare at the picture of my kids on the nightstand and whisper a muddled promise that I won't go this way. I have better ideas.

But I came close, and this wasn't the first time.

I lay there a while, and then, before the pain hits, I lift myself from the bed and roll the awful thing in the quilt and then roll it out again into the toilet. I clean the caked shit and blood off my ass with wet paper towels and soap. Ointment on my prolapsed rectum, and the painful easing of it back inside of me. Then I shove the whole stinking quilt and the towels in a giant black trash bag and seal it with a bulky knot. I toss it by the door. I'll put it in the dumpster later, and no one will know.

And now, my body is coming alive. The pain hits as it does. I swallow a tall glass of water and crawl back into bed, pulling the sheet over me. The pain is full on me, now.

I feel clutched in the hard claw of Death.

I spend long hours in the bed, curled into myself, wishing the pain away, to no avail. It hammers away at my spinning head and quivers in my upturned guts. It swells the marrow in my bones and twists the tendons of my limbs. And it conjures the memories of the night past; the frustration, the failure, the beating and my impotence on the sidewalk, the gun in my pocket, rendered useless by my lack of will, and the finality of everything.

At one in the afternoon I'm awakened by the doorbell, followed by urgent raps on the door. I must have fallen asleep again. I lay there, waiting to be called, but there is no call. I hear receding footsteps. I pray there isn't something wrong with my kids or my mother, because I can't get up. I stretch out and grab my phone. No messages. I hold it to my chest for a while, waiting, but none come. So it was nothing important at the door. Maybe just a package; although I'm not expecting one.

I sit up and take stock. I'm faint, and dizzy, but I think the worst has passed. I look to the window and see flurries drifting past through the spaces between the blinds. I pull myself up on shaky legs and peer out the window. About six inches of snow covers everything. The sky is pressing down like a gray lid. The world looks small.

I pull on a tee shirt and sweat pants and make for the living room and collapse on the sofa. That's as far as I can go. It's not just the hangover and the aches from getting punched out and kicked, it's the loss of blood. The gun lies before me on the coffee table, broken open. The box of shells is spilled beside it. I can see I have added the fifth round, although I don't remember doing so. I pick up the gun and look it over, and anxiously scan the walls, the floor, the furniture, wondering if I fired off a round and don't remember that either. I don't see any holes in the wall. And it occurs to me that if I had, someone would have heard the shot and called the cops. Or, maybe not, with all the drinkers in the building. By the time I got home everyone else could have been passed out. I consider this for a while. I don't think I fired the gun. I think I would have remembered doing that. It finally occurs to me to check the cylinder for an empty casing. There are none.

So now I have five rounds in the gun. Two more and I'm ready.

I box up the loose shells and put it all away behind the liquor bottles. I open the front door to look for a package and breathe the cold, fresh air. There is no package. But the air makes me feel a little better.

I lay on the couch for a while. I know I need to see what I wrote to Johanna, but I'm not ready for that, yet.

An hour later the doorbell rings again. A man calls my name. Maybe there is trouble.

"I'm coming," I shout.

I open the door and a frowning old guy in a parka is standing on the stoop. He asks me my name. I tell him.

"I have a summons to appear for you," he barks, and slaps a brown oversized envelope in my hand. Then he turns on his heel and hurries away and climbs into a tiny, idling car and drives carefully away, spitting chunks of snow in his wake.

"What?"

A summons? What the fuck did I do? Is this about the fight at the bar? But they don't know who I am, how could they send me a summons?

Did that menage-a-whore Debra give them my name? Why?

Then I think of my wallet and my ID. Did I leave it somewhere? But there it is, on the floor where I tossed it when I came in last night. I pick it up and rifle through it. Nothing is missing, except all the money I spent.

I sit down and tear open the envelope. A subpoena from Family Court. I have to appear on some date regarding non-payment of child support.

"Fuck."

I've barely paid my ex-wife anything in the past year. She hasn't given me a hard time about it, she knows I'm broke. So I'm surprised at her sudden leap from understanding to subpoena. I want to talk to her, but not now. I'm too fucked up.

I'm hungry. It's nearly three already. I hope I can stomach something. I start the coffee pot. When it starts to gurgle, I'm suddenly ravenous.

I crave meat. I always do when I'm hung over, and I don't know why. I mix up four eggs in a bowl and let them sit while I fry up four strips of turkey bacon in a fry pan. I take the bacon out before it crisps. I like it chewy. I pour the eggs in the pan, over the bacon grease, and while they sizzle I stick a few frozen sausage links in the microwave. In two minutes everything is ready; I don't like hard eggs, either, and slide them onto the plate the moment they're barely tight. I pour a small bowl full of bran flakes, a glass of orange juice, and fill a mug with coffee.

I'm mad with the scent and sight of it all. I squirt ketchup and hot sauce on the eggs and tear into the food.

It's so good, at first. But about halfway through I feel sick and can't stomach any more of the meat or the eggs. My insides are jumping and threatening to blow. I steady myself with a few spoons of bran flakes, then push it all away and keep to the juice and the coffee. I have a vague urge for a cigarette, but I know from experience a smoke at this point would only make me sicker.

I start up the laptop to see the weather and the news and eventually, the email to Johanna. But halfway through the coffee I nearly shit my pants, and have to run to the toilet. A flood of diarrhea pours out of me with a stink that turns my stomach. But, at least there is no blood.

Maybe I bled to death and there's nothing left to come out of ass, I think, and laugh quietly to myself.

I glance through a book on WWII tank battles while I wait a half an hour for the remaining reluctant scraps to clear themselves from my colon. Then I'm done, and consider myself lucky: I dropped most of my load while I slept and it cost me a quilt, but it was the fastest shitting I've done in in a long time.

I see my haggard face in the mirror while I wash. Pale skin, stubbled cheeks; hollow, bloodshot eyes. Swollen, where the guy hit me. A bruise on my jaw.

Afterwards, I call my ex-wife.

"Hey," I say.

"How are you?"

"Surprised. I got the summons today."

"Yeah. Well, I'm sorry, but it can't go on forever. I really need some money from you. And you owe me a lot."

Her husband isn't working. I'm not sure whether he was fired, laid off, or quit, but he isn't.

"I know. You know the story. I'm just surprised you took the legal route."

"Well, I don't see any other recourse. And there's more."

"What more?"

"I'm not going to let you see the kids until I see some money."

"Come on! This isn't like you at all. And that's only going to hurt them."

"I know, but it's the only leverage I have."

"Well, you're taking me to court. That's a lot of leverage."

"Yeah, well maybe we can avoid court. But in the meantime, I'm cutting you off for a while."

"That won't stand, you know. Just because I don't pay doesn't mean I can't see the kids. If I challenge that you'll lose."

"I probably will. But I do have custody, so until then, I can do it."

"I can't see them at all?"

"Not for a while. Look, I hate to do it, but I think it's the only way I'll get you to do anything about this."

"This sounds like the same bullshit my mother pulled when I was unemployed. She suddenly quit helping me out. 'I'm not going to send you any more money until you get a job', as if I laid myself off on purpose. As if I'm deliberately holding out on you now."

"I think you could do something if you really tried."

"Sure I can. Can I at least talk to them? Like, every couple of days?"

"Of course. And I explained the situation to them."

"So they'll know it's all my fault."

"I didn't word it that way."

"Whatever. Just put them on the phone. Then I'm signing off."

I wait while she gets the kids. And, I think, it doesn't matter. Two more bullets to load and everything will change.

My son comes on.

"Hi Dad."

We chat for a while. I apologize. He understands and isn't mad at me. I tell him I love him, and then he passes the phone to my daughter.

"Hi Daddy," she says.

"Hi, sweetie."

"Pay mommy the money soon, because I miss you."

"I will, soon as I can."

Now I'm getting choked up. I have to get off the phone fast. I tell her I love her and then I hang up.

Fuck.

Maybe it's better this way.

I don't know.

While I'm this fucked up, I figure I might as well see what I wrote to Johanna so I don't have to get upset all over again later.

Kind of like a two-for-one special at the Agony Cafe.

As I suspected, I replied to Johanna's brush-off with a drunken, whimpering plea for her to come back to me and give us another chance. It's pathetic and I'm disgusted with myself. I wish I could take it back, but it's too late. And she hasn't replied.

The snow has stopped. The Dudes are shoveling out their cars. Snow plows are slowly clearing the road. The guy across the street is making a snowman with his little girls. I think of the plastic saucers and toboggan in the closet, and it hurts to know I won't be taking my kids sledding this weekend.

I clean up the kitchen, straighten the furniture I knocked awry last night, and lay down on the sofa. There's nothing else to do.

After a while I want a cigarette, and think I can stomach one, but I don't want to go outside and have to talk to anyone. I don't want to stand there watching the guy across the street playing with his kids.

I load the sixth round in the gun and fall asleep.

* * *

When I wake up its five-thirty, and it's dark out. Maybe more snow is coming. Not that it matters to me.

I'm shaky and wrung out, but I'm okay. I'm hungry again, so I have a couple of hot dogs and a can of beets. I crap again, for a short half-hour, and read my book. I take a shower.

I log on to the laptop. No reply from Johanna. I look for a while at the book I've been writing, on and off, for the past year.

A story about being unemployed. It's a mess. I close the file. That's done. It's eight o'clock.

Now what to do?

I take out the gun and hold it in my hand and think for a long time.

It's nine-thirty.

I put the gun away.

I get up and pick out some clothes. I check how much is left in my bank account. I dress.

I'm going out.

*   *   *

Despite the snow, there are people out on the Strip, moving from bar to bar. But the girls just aren't as interesting in their snow boots, long coats, and hats. A few are making wobbly attempts on the icy sidewalks in heels; they cling to friends and shriek the way girls do when they're drunk and about to fall.

I withdraw forty dollars from my bank's ATM on the corner. It's enough; I don't plan on getting drunk. I just need to get out and have a taste. It's a moot point: less than ten dollars remains in my account.

My cell phone rings, but I don't recognize the number. I wait for a voice mail. One appears, so I retrieve it. It's from Rich in Systems.

"Hey douchebag, your fucking job failed again. It put out some error messages. Call me back and tell me what to do, numb nuts."

"Fuck it," I say, and delete the voicemail. I don't care about work anymore. I light a cigarette and head for the Lizard. After I go a block a pair of young girls stops me.

"Hey, can we bum a cigarette?"

I look them over. They're cute in their hooded parkas, with their flushed red cheeks.

Fuck them in their hooded parkas.

"No, you can't," I say, and keep walking. A few seconds pass, which I surmise they spent in dumb incomprehension, and then I hear them squawk in indignation. I'm tempted to shout back at them, but I keep my mouth shut.

"Imagine that, you little twats" I whisper, "you couldn't charm a guy into giving you something for nothing."

I finish my smoke outside the Lizard and toss it onto the icy pavement that gleams in the light of the street lamps. I go inside and find a spot at the bar. There's just a small crowd tonight. A DJ with a karaoke machine is on the stage, imploring people to come up and try a song. There are no takers. He puts on some Springsteen. A bartender comes over, and I order a vodka tonic. She brings it; I pay her, and sip it slowly.

I notice the Crossdresser is here tonight; a fixture on the Strip, he's a skinny old guy in Coke-bottle glasses who wanders in and out of the bars wearing leather pants, women's boots and blouses, and a wig of flowing white curls. On holidays he accessorizes accordingly: draping strings of red and green blinking lights over himself for Christmas and New Year's, leprechaun hat and green shirt and boots for St. Patrick's Day, and a red, white and blue ensemble and a sparkling pinwheel on the Fourth of July. He wanders around the bars, chats up all the girls, and dances for hours. A lot of girls come out on the floor and dance with him. He often turns around, bends over and gyrates his ass at them. I suppose he wants them to fuck him with a strap-on. I talked to him once; I was drunk and impressed with his antics.

"I gotta give you credit, man," I shouted in his ear, "you just do your thing and don't give a shit what anybody thinks."

"You only have one life," he replied, "and you have to live it your way."

I saw him in the day time last summer, when I was unemployed and out riding my bike. He passed me on the road, driving a wheezing pickup truck filled with brush and tree cuttings. His skinny arms stuck out like white sticks from the cutoff sleeves of a tattered checkered shirt. His face had a desperate, angry look to it. He raced past as if being chased, and disappeared down the next cross street, hopping the corner curb with his rear wheel.

I finish my drink and order another. The deejay still has no takers for karaoke. He keeps playing Springsteen, in alternating order: one Bruce song, then something else, then Bruce again. The deejay is an older guy, probably forty. Only an old guy would play that much Springsteen in a bar like this. Although there are some fortyish people here tonight: a group of about ten guys and girls, evenly split. They could be married couples, or just a big group of friends. They're getting into the Springsteen. So is the Crossdresser.

I feel my phone vibrate in my pocket. I look at the incoming number. It's Rich from Systems again. I send the call straight to voicemail.

The bar is slowly filling up. The people have to have their fun, snow and ice be damned.

Two drinks down. I feel dizzy and wrung out. I don't know why I'm here, except that I don't want to stay home. I suppose that's a good enough reason. I order another vodka and tonic. Maybe this will be my last one tonight. We'll see.

I step out for a cigarette, pulling long and slow down to the butt. It goes straight to my throat and burns, and I have a coughing fit. A pack of young girls goes into the bar, but none of them ask me for a cigarette. But they piss me off, anyway.

Back inside there's a roar that takes me a few seconds to identify. It's one of the fortyish guys up on stage, trying to sing *Girls, Girls, Girls.* And of course the forty-something women are going nuts, shaking their asses and hopping all over the dance floor. Some of the young girls join in—even though they're barely older than the song—but everybody knows the song nowadays. Poison sold it, along with the rest of their hits, to market some kind of product. And now Brett Michaels is on TV, closing the deal: The Great Resuscitation of 80s pop-metal schlock culture and its flat-lined rock stars.

But then I think, so what, who cares, the girls are having fun making fools of themselves.

Look what I was doing, just last night.

Fourth drink. It goes down easy. Fifth drink in hand. I can do anything, now. But what to do?

Another guy keeps with the Poison and belts out *Talk Dirty to Me.* He's awful, but the music carries the dancers along. When he's finally done, the deejay nearly pushes him from the stage. The guy is drunk and smiling like a dope. He takes a bow. The crowd applauds.

I've had enough. I'm on stage, now. "Give me the fucking mike," I tell the deejay, "I'm sick of this crap. We need some real music."

"OK, pal, don't get excited. Whaddaya wanna sing?"

"You got any Doors?"

"Doors? Somewhere."

"Gimme Roadhouse Blues. I'll show these morons about music."

And a moment later I'm belting out,

> *Oh, keep your eyes on the road,*
>
> *your hands upon the wheel*
>
> *Yeah, we're goin' to the Roadhouse*
>
> *We're gonna have a real good time*

And the crowd stares in shock for a moment--because I can actually sing. My voice is deep and rough and all the smoking and drinking has finished it with a bluesy tone. Or so I convince myself. But I can carry a simple tune, and I'm loud. It's good enough for the drunks, and the crowd goes nuts, cheering, clapping, rocking out. The forty-somethings are particularly captivated, of course. They grew up with the song.

I do the best Jim Morrison that I can, twisting, shouting, groaning, sexing it up. I'm drunk now too, after all. The women love it, along with the Crossdresser, who joins them on the dance floor, shaking his thing and bending over for them.

Well, I woke up this morning, got myself a beer

Yeah, I woke up this morning, got myself a beer

The future's uncertain and the end is always near

Let it roll, baby roll. All night long. All fucking night. Yeah.

The song is done, but the crowd wants more. They're applauding, howling, stamping their feet. The sweating girls look up to me expectantly, they're not finished dancing. The deejay motions for me to go on.

"Gimme more Doors," I shout at him.

"Sure! Whaddaya want, Jim?"

I think for a second. Then it hits me like I'm cumming.

"Back Door Man."

I follow the third note with a long, arching howl. The girls on the dance floor burst into screams once they figure out what I'm doing. This is for them, and they know it. The Crossdresser would like to think so, too, and he continues his bent-over act, but instead of bending over for the girls, he wiggles his skinny ass up near the stage and bends over for me.

The women and the girls follow his lead. They crowd the lip of the stage at my feet, shaking their asses and bending over for me. I scream my way through the song as loud as I can, barely coherent, drawing out the words in a long orgasm of sound. It occurs to me that if there was ever a way to fuck ten women all at once, this is it, and there they are, offering themselves before me. I nearly blow the finish, laughing over it.

Then it's over, and there are all these desiring eyes and big asses waiting for more. For me, to take them. I just have to reach out and choose. Maybe.

In the electric hum, the deejay shouts to me.

"You missed your calling, man."

I look over the women. And the Crossdresser, who is just as beguiled.

"So," I cry, "you want a back door man?"

They scream, yes, yes.

"You want me to be your back door man?"

Yes, yes.

"You do, huh?" I shout, and point at the Crossdresser. "Well, I'd rather fuck this guy's dried up old ass than any of your stinking twats! Go home to your husbands, your fiancées, your boyfriends and your children, you fucking drunken whores! You fucking…"

But that's the last thing I get to say because the deejay cuts the power to the mike and two big bouncers grab me by the arms and one claps his palm over my mouth. They hoist me off the floor and race to the door, past all the furious and indignant eyes and beyond the outraged shouts. I'm thrashing in their grip and kicking air with my feet but they're too strong. Then I'm out in the cold air and they toss me into the pile of plowed black snow lining the curb.

"You better get the fuck out of here before those bitches come outside and rip off your balls," one says, his tone more sympathetic than angry. He takes my arm and pulls me to my feet before heading back inside.

I take his advice, and hurry down the street, brushing the snow from my jacket. I light a cigarette on the run.

I turn a corner and start to laugh. I'm happy, and satisfied. That piece of business is finished.

I'm free.

But when I step inside my empty apartment, the feeling gives way to silence and emptiness.

There is nothing more to do tonight. I piss, brush my teeth, and go to bed.

In the dark I furtively masturbate into one of the old gym socks I keep under the pillow for that purpose. When I cum, I give out a loud sob. I yank off the sock, wipe myself, and toss it into the blackness of the room. Sleep comes, and to my surprise, I don't dream.

VII.

It's Sunday. I sleep until the ring of the cell phone awakens me. It's Carl. I don't answer. It's just after ten. I lay there until the voice mail alert shows, and then I listen.

"Hey, it's Carl. I know it's the weekend but Rich has been trying to reach you about the file job, it failed. Did you get his messages? We gotta get it fixed or they're going to flip out at the home office. Give me a call when you get this, thanks."

Poor Carl. He has to put up with a lot of shit. But I'm not going to call back. It's all over and it doesn't matter anymore.

I lay in bed for a while until hunger drives me to my feet. I'm a bit weak, and tired, but I'm not hung over. What did I have last night, five drinks? That's nothing.

I feel like I need to get my strength back, and make myself feel good. It's all about the body, today. I don't want to think. My mind has gone limp. I want to eat, and take care of the body, today.

I peer outside. The pale sun glows dimly behind a gray veil of clouds. The half-foot of snow lays heavy on the ground. Nothing moves in the yard or on the street. Everyone in the building is probably half-drunk and still asleep. Across the street, my neighbor's wife is probably making pancakes for the kids. The woods beyond the cul-de-sac appear undisturbed save for a single bird, hopping along the saddle of the ridge of plowed snow lining the buried curb.

I put on the coffee. While it's brewing, I put together a huge breakfast: three over-easy eggs, with salt and pepper and fried slow and soft, laid on toast; a half package of bacon, a bowl of oatmeal, and orange juice. I settle down with it and enjoy it, slowly. I eat most of the oatmeal first, and then alternate between the eggs and the bacon. I work on one toast and egg combination at a time, pulling away and eating the whites first, then popping the yolk so it soaks into the toast. Then I cut the toast into small squares, top each with a folded bacon strip, and chew it slowly, savoring the blend of taste and texture.

The body feels good when it's all done.

I take my coffee outside to sip with a cigarette. It's not as cold as I thought. I'm comfortable wrapped in a sweater, my leather coat, and the coffee warming me. I toss the smoldering butt, finish the coffee inside, drink some more, and go for a crap when I'm finished. I'm content to sit there and read my World War II book and let it come however it may come. I get into the book. It's interesting. It keeps me from thinking.

After an hour, I'm done. Some blood, but not enough to be concerned. I make the necessary corrections to my unraveled colon, clean up, and realize it's already after noon.

I still want to feel good.

I log on to my laptop, but I avoid my email account, the news, the weather, and go straight for the porno sites. I get some oil, some paper towels, and, discarding my pants, browse and pleasure myself. After an hour I pause to turn up the heat because my bare legs are cold. The heat comes up quickly and I keep going until four o'clock, when I can't hold back any longer and cum all over the towels. I sit for a while in the aftermath, dazed, until I've gone completely limp. Then I take a hot shower and clean off the mess.

The apartment has gone dark when I come out. I turn on a few lights, just enough to see, but not enough to wake the place up. I dress in the wet steam of the bathroom to trap the warmth under my clothes. Carl has called again while I was in the shower. He says that he got someone else to look at the job, but to call him anyway.

I'm hungry again, this time for something simple. I cook up some pasta and marinara sauce and slowly eat an overloaded plate of it.

While sipping on my coffee in the bloated, hazy aftermath of my dinner, my brain switches on, and I feel everything drop into a bottomless, black pit.

I look at my email, and there's a message from Johanna waiting for me. I read it.

She doesn't understand what I'm trying to do, but it's all over and done for us. To mark it with an incontestable mark of finality, she closes with the revelation that she's with someone else now.

So it's truly over and done.

I take out the gun and load the seventh round. Now the chamber is full, and it's finally ready to use. Seven rounds in seven days. I promised myself if things came to seven rounds in seven days, I would use it. And now it has. And I will.

I hold the gun in my hand. I sink into the easy chair, shaking with the knowledge of how it will be the tool to make my final mark, tomorrow.

I don't sleep well, this time.

*   *   *

Break on through to the other side

I wake up early, although there is no need to hurry. I can take all the time I like.

No I can't. It has to be today.

Why shower? There's no need. But I do, anyway, because I want to feel clean. Why eat? Because I'm hungry. But just a light breakfast, today.

I'm shaking from a night tormented by awful dreams and hollow pains of heartbreak. And regrets; I feel bad for Carl and Rich and all of them, for never calling back and for abandoning them.

I'm not as callous and hard as I thought I would be when this day would come. I'm shaking and brittle and afraid.

I'm not of the Mt. Suribachi generation, for certain.

But I have to steel myself. I've got to get out of here; I have some stops to make.

When I'm finally ready I throw on my coat and take out the gun. I check to load, spin the chamber, carefully cock the hammer and then slowly let it retract. Then I stuff it deep in my jacket pocket and head out the door. I pass the girls next door, brushing Friday's snow from their cars, and answer their Hellos with a slight nod. I sit in my idling car until they're gone, and then I clean it off. When I'm done I get settled into the warm seat, switch the dehumidifier to heat, adjust the fan, adjust the vents, check the mirrors, and fiddle with the seat.

"Just go already."

I put the car in gear and for the first few moments it's like I'm driving for the first time. But I calm down a bit, and consider my route. Still efficient, and conscious of economy, I decide to go out to my furthest destination first and then work my way back.

I pull on to the highway and head for my ex-wife's house. I should make it before my kids leave for school.

I float along the highway like on a cloud. The sun holds sway today, and I'm reminded of being on an airliner and breaking free of the overcast into the bright sky above.

Alongside the highway, the snow is beginning to melt. I race past, lightheaded and short of breath.

I leave the highway, kicking up a fan of spray, and take a roundabout route to my ex-wife's street. I don't want to pass them on the road if they've already left for school.

I park on a rise on the cross-street near my ex-wife's house where I have a clear, if dim, view of it. Her car is still in the drive. I sit, and wait, with the engine running and my heart racing. Soon, I need air. I crack the windows an inch.

After a few minutes, they emerge: my son, my daughter, and my ex-wife, all fixing their coats. The kids are hauling backpacks. My ex-wife urges them into the car. They don't look my way. If they did they would see the pale, horrid face I glimpse in the rearview mirror before I turn away from it. And the white bones of my knuckles as I squeeze the wheel, fighting for control.

They get in the car and after a moment's idling, drive off to school. Once they're out of sight, I deflate, without and within. I can't say the words I should say to them, the words they can't hear anyway.

I give them a few moments lead and then I go. I cross the highway, pick up a secondary road, and shortly find myself in the corporate park where I work. I pull into the parking lot of my building. It's still early, and there are few cars. Huge mounds of plowed snow line the circumference of the lot and rivulets of ice are draining from beneath them.

I sit for a while, while the cars drift into the lot, one at time, and I gaze at the place I worked at these past years. Where my fate was made, sealed, and handed back to me, along with everyone else's.

What a sad injustice. What a waste.

There's no sense in staying any longer, because there's nothing left to say or feel about this place. I start the car, and just then, Ted pulls up alongside me. He rolls down the window.

"Hey, what the fuck is up with you? Drunk all weekend?"

"What? What do you mean?"

"They've been calling you all weekend about your job, it failed! Didn't you get the messages?"

"It doesn't matter," I say.

"Aren't you coming in?"

"No."

"What's the matter with you? Are you sick?"

"You know what it is."

"What are you talking about?"

"You know. I got all the hints you dropped."

"What? What hints?"

"Don't bullshit me. I'm not coming in. And I'm not coming back."

"Are you fucking crazy? Do you want to get fired? What the fuck are you up to? You don't look well, do you need a doctor?"

Does he really not know? Did I misinterpret everything he said last week?

"Yeah, I'm kinda sick. That's why I didn't pick up the phone this weekend. I'm gonna go to the doctor today."

"So what are you doing here?"

"I had to get something."

"What's wrong?"

"Nothing. I'm just sick."

"What the fuck are you up to?"

"Nothing, I'm just sick. I'm going now." I put the car in gear.

"Hey, wait! Wait! Promise me you'll go to the doctor."

"I just told you I'm going."

"Promise me. Go right now, go to the ER."

"I don't need to go to the ER."

"Yes, you do. Promise me you'll go, and that you'll call me later."

"OK, I promise. I'll go, and I'll call you later."

"You mean it?"

"Yes."

"I should take you."

"No, I can drive. I drove here, didn't I?"

"You gonna keep your promise?"

"Yes."

"If you don't I'm gonna kick you skinny little ass, understand?"

"OK. Catch you later."

"Hey!"

"What?"

"Don't forget…I wanna take you and the kids fishing."

"OK."

I drive away as quick as I can. I look in the rearview mirror before I turn from the lot and I see Ted, standing beside his car, hands in his coat pockets, watching me.

I'm very confused driving home. Maybe I should listen to Ted and go to the hospital. He said I look sick. Am I really sick? Why is he so concerned? Why did he have to remind me about taking my kids out on his boat?

I should keep my promise to him, and not just because he'll kick my ass if I don't. I should go to the hospital. It would be easy. The hospital is only a half mile from my apartment.

But no, that would solve nothing and only make things worse. Nothing would change. I would still be me and things would still be what they are.

I pull into the parking lot of my building. I should really be on my way to the park, to hike out to the lake, but I'm stalling. It has to be done today, and not here.

Well, what's another hour or so?

It's a nice day, and warming up. I feel like a coffee. Why not a coffee? A walk uptown—it's a beautiful town in the daytime—get a cup of good coffee from the coffee shop. I start walking through the narrow lane of pavement shoveled from the sidewalk.

I have the courage to do this, I know now. To go to the park, hike around the lake, up the trail into the woods and then behind the great fallen oak and put the gun to my temple and pull the trigger and put an end to all this pain and hopelessness. To mark the end of things in a pleasant place and be found there by a stranger. And not in my apartment, or in my car, where, God forbid, my kids or my mother might find me. That would be too much for them.

Yes, I can do it, now. Seven rounds for seven days of hell. That was the deal I made with myself. Now I have to close the deal.

The early-morning crowd is all at work and the coffee shop is nearly empty. Just the guy at the counter, an old man at a table, and a young, thin girl on the sofa, texting.

It's Melissa.

I stand there, staring at her. The guy at the counter asks me twice for my order.

"Never mind," I say.

I sit down beside her. She turns.

"Remember me?" I whisper.

"Holy shit. Of course I do. How are you?"

"Not so good. How are you? What are you doing in town?"

"I'm here for a job. But what's wrong? You look awful."

I tell her about my kids, and my job, and I tell her about Johanna. But I don't tell her about the gun or anything else.

"Oh my god. You're still all fucked up over that girl?"

"I just can't get over her."

Melissa turns away and looks out at the street. There is a long silence, and then she turns back to me, and stares at me intently.

"I have to tell you something," she says.

*   *   *

Melissa passes out the door and into the street, turns, and gives me a small wave through the glass. Then she's gone.

At that moment, the cacophony in my head erupts in one last crashing note like the finale of a symphony conducted by a madman. A demonic symphony I wasn't even aware was playing. Only the sudden silence has brought it to my attention. And I swear I can hear the fading ring of the last strike made on the cymbals. Then it's gone.

I leave the coffee shop in the opposite direction of Melissa. I head towards home. Johanna works in a small office on a side street halfway there. I'm going to stop and see her.

Johanna's car is the only one in the parking lot; her colleagues must be out on sales calls. I pause for a moment on the street, out of sight of the office, and then I stride across the lot and through the door.

Johanna is sitting at her small desk in the reception area, working on her computer. She looks up at me and her face pales. I sit down in the chair before her desk, hands buried in my pockets.

"Hi," I say.

She looks me over. She doesn't know what to say. She coughs.

"Didn't you get my email yesterday?" she says.

"Yes, but that's not why I'm here."

"OK. Then, why?"

"You'll never guess who I just ran into at the coffee shop."

"I don't know. Who?"

"Melissa."

"Melissa? Who's Melissa?"

"You don't remember? She's the prostitute you hired off the internet to pick me up and fuck me in her car."

Now Johanna turns red.

"What? I don't know what you're talking about!"

"Don't lie to me. She still has your phone number and your credit card number in her address book. She showed me."

Johanna's chest rises and falls in a rapid sequence, her nostrils flare, and she glares at me.

"Well, you fucked her, didn't you? You cheated on me, didn't you?"

"I fucked her all right, but as for cheating, I don't think so, since you arranged it—and you did break up with me that night. But however you want to look at it, I came clean about it, and I was sorry. But you haven't, and you aren't. How come a whore can come clean with me, and you can't?"

Johanna says nothing. The redness fades, and she goes pale again.

"So why did you trap me like that?"

She looks away.

"I know why. You did it to get back at me for the mean

things I said about you in that email you weren't supposed to read. So you had to make me ashamed, and guilty, and make me suffer for it. "

She doesn't answer.

"And to absolve yourself of any blame for what happened and get all the sympathy, so you could tell your family and all your friends that I cheated on you."

She fixes a glaring look on me.

"All right then. I wanted to get back at you. Especially for how you thought you were such hot shit that you could get other women and that you didn't need me. Well, turns out you were wrong. You think you're hot shit because you fucked some little twenty-something bitch, but it wasn't you, it was me who made it happen."

I leap to my feet and start screaming.

"You want to ruin me, don't you? Just because I bruised your fucking precious little ego with some words you weren't even supposed to read. And you're not even sorry!"

"No, I'm not! You don't know how much you hurt me, you bastard!"

I lunge and grab Johanna with both fists and pull her across the desk to me. She throws weak punches at my head and twists her face from mine like from a hissing flame. I shake her brutally and she leaps in my grip like a dancing marionette.

"It's not losing my job, or losing my kids, or the drinking or the fucked up women or running out of money that's destroying me, it's you! You! "

I tighten my grip on her with my left hand and with my right I pull the revolver from my pocket and wave it in her face. Her eyes bulge in fear and she fights to get away. But I don't let go.

"I was going to finish myself off with this, but I'm gonna let you do it! That's what you want, don't you? To destroy me?" I reverse the gun and force it into her right hand so it's pointing at me. She starts to scream. With both hands I struggle against her wild thrashings to tighten her grip on the handle and work her index finger around the trigger.

She's crying now. "No, no, stop, stop it, please!"

I pull her hand and the gun to my face and point it right between my eyes.

"This is what you want, Johanna, so just do it!"

Then the gun goes off.

*   *   *

I've been out of jail about six months now. I served half of a four-year sentence. I was released early for good behavior. Plus, I think the parole board felt sorry for me, a skinny white middle-aged guy, tossed in the snake pit. I was beaten up a few times in there. And a few other things. They probably saved my life, letting me out early.

Before jail, I was in the hospital for a few weeks. And not just for getting half my right ear shot off and my eardrum ruptured. I had to be observed to see if I was fit for trial.

I did jail time mainly for having the gun. And I guess for going a little crazy.

I'm not sure what really happened, how I got shot like I did. Did Johanna manage to yank the gun from my face at the last second? Or did I change my mind and push her arm aside just in time?

Who pulled the trigger? I think I did, and she testified as much.

But I'm not so sure.

I wonder about it sometimes. But it doesn't really matter, anymore.

When I was released I came back to town. Some things have changed, and most of the people I know are gone. Johanna spent a year in therapy and then moved away. But some things are the same. Like the Strip. It's still the same scene I left behind.

I work on the Strip, at the small pub with the silent bartender. He owns the place now, and did remember my good tips. So he gave me a job. I clean up after closing, five nights a week. I take out the empty bottles, the trash, clean the bar top, the tables, and mop and wax the floor. I'm usually done by dawn. It's nice, I suppose. I get to see a lot of sunrises.

The drunk kids, the hot young girls, the Milfs…they're all still out on the Strip. I get uptown at closing time and watch them. They don't have much effect on me anymore. Just a faint yearning like a phone ringing in a house heard passing by on the street. There's a bit of a stronger feeling when I come upon couples humping in the grass behind the recycle bins out back of the pub. If they see me, I shoo them away. If they don't, I just tiptoe back into the bar and stay away until they're done.

The job is only about twenty hours a week, and doesn't pay much. I can buy some food, clothes, shoes…I have a used bicycle. I don't drink anymore…I got cleaned up in jail…but I do smoke. That's all I can afford. I still have my bathroom problems. I use the bar toilet in the morning after I'm done working. By the time my boss comes to open up, I'm long gone. But for any business later in the day, or on my days off, it's hard.

My kids came around a few times to see me. They're both in high school; they have part-time jobs and my son drives now. I know they're embarrassed and ashamed to be seen with me, their bum father with his mutilated ear and his rotting teeth. They take me out to the diner. We pick at our food and don't say much. But I enjoy seeing them. I'm sure their mother makes them come to see me. And I'm sure that once they're older, they will stop.

I'm sleeping in the woods past the cul-de-sac. I fixed up a lean-to over a mattress I found at the curb. I dug a fire pit. It's all hidden in the midst of a cluster of thorn bushes. I feel safe, and have privacy here…nobody comes in the woods. I guess the word got out that a crazy man is back here.

I've been lucky, out here. It's been a long, warm autumn. Winter is coming soon. I'm not worried. I can get a coat from the Salvation Army.

But my ear bothers me. It itches and I pick at it and now it's infected. It won't heal. The open wound draws flies that lay their eggs deep inside. They've hatched and the maggot offspring are driving me mad, crawling around in there.

But the worst thing is, they make sounds. They speak.

In Johanna's voice.

THE END

Alan Wynzel has been a storyteller and writer from a very young age. In the sixth grade he wrote a sixty-three page WWII story. He's lived in New Jersey all of his life except for a brief flirtation in Lawrence, Kansas in the early 90s, where he started writing seriously. (His girlfriend told him he'd never make it with a guitar, please write instead— she liked her peace and quiet). Since then he's written six novels, including THE SEVENTH ROUND, and his childhood memoir. THE SEVENTH ROUND is his first work to be published. Now he's writing screenplays, having adapted his latest novel, a WWII drama, into a feature length script. Much of THE SEVENTH ROUND is true, or extrapolated from truth. Especially the sex—all true. But Mr. Wynzel wants it to go on record that he has never owned a gun, never got into a bar fight, and most of all, has never sang Karaoke.